# CONTACT MR. DELGADO

English adventurer Harvey Landon agrees to help his old Oxford friend, Don Vargas, who is plotting the overthrow of a South American government. However, the Revolutionaries are without aircraft, and to obtain their supply, Landon volunteers to take a letter out of the country to a mysterious Mr. Delgado in New York. Complications begin as Landon is stalked on board the New York-bound oil-tanker by two agents intent on killing him and stealing the letter.

# JAMES PATTINSON

◆

# CONTACT
# MR. DELGADO

*Complete and Unabridged*

# ULVERSCROFT
*Leicester*

First published in Great Britain

First Large Print Edition
published September 1994

241357

British Library CIP Data

Pattinson, James
    Contact Mr. Delgado.—Large print ed.—
Ulverscroft large print series: adventure & suspense
I. Title
823.914 [F]


ISBN 0–7089–3155–3

Published by
F. A. Thorpe (Publishing) Ltd.
Anstey, Leicestershire
Set by Words & Graphics Ltd.
Anstey, Leicestershire
Printed and bound in Great Britain by
T. J. Press (Padstow) Ltd., Padstow, Cornwall

This book is printed on acid-free paper

# 1

## In Gaol

HARVEY LANDON was arrested at half-past ten in the morning and taken to the Santa Ana police-station. An iron door clanged shut behind him, a key grated in the lock, and not for the first time in the forty-one years of his chequered life Landon found himself a prisoner.

He felt dirty, thirsty, and humiliated. There was a smear of blood on his chin, a bruise on his left cheek, and a pain in his right shoulder which was aggravated when he moved his arm. His shirt was torn, and his toes throbbed. The police had not handled him gently, perhaps resenting his attempts to escape. They had struck him in the face, wrenched his arm, trodden on his toes with their heavy boots. He had been a fool to come into Santa Ana at all; but Don Diego had said it would be safe.

1

'No one in the town knows you. No one knows that you are one of my men.'

Landon remembered the words, and his thin lips twisted. Some one had known him; some one had given him away. Santa Ana had been very far from safe.

"A cigarette, señor. One cigarette, for the love of Mary."

The voice came suddenly from a heap of rags lying on the floor, startling Landon. He looked at the heap and saw two shining black eyes staring up at him from a villainous, unshaven face.

"A cigarette to save a poor man's life. A cigarette to relieve the sufferings of the wretched."

Landon felt in the pocket of his jacket, found a packet of cigarettes, tossed one to the heap of rags, which caught it skilfully, and took one for himself. He struck a match and bent down over his companion in captivity. A stench of sweat and dirt, alcohol and bad breath, came up to meet him, filling him with disgust. The man on the floor leered wolfishly, revealing brown, stained teeth.

2

"You suffer misfortune too, señor."

"Yes."

Landon rested his shoulders against the whitewashed wall of the room and drew smoke into his lungs, not desiring to talk. He wondered what Don Diego would do, whether he could expect help. Diego would know what had happened, for Pedro had escaped, and he would carry the news. It would remain for Diego to take what action he thought fit.

He let the smoke come slowly from his mouth and watched it drifting up towards the rough plaster of the ceiling. The room was some ten feet by twenty, the common prison in which all awaiting trial or interrogation were confined. It had brick walls, no furniture of any kind, two barred, unglazed windows above head height, and an earthen floor rammed hard by the trampling of many feet.

The wall in which the windows were situated formed one side of a narrow street, little more than an alley. Landon could hear the occasional *clop* of hoofs as horses or mules passed by his prison, snatches of song, a man's voice raised in anger, a burst of laughter. The knowledge

3

that free men were passing so close to him aggravated the bitterness of captivity, seeming to mock him. The reek of urine came up from the floor, biting at his nostrils. He stabbed the earth with his toe, filled with anger and frustration. How long would they keep him here? How long before they sent him on to Cuenca or San Antonio — to a travesty of a trial, to a prison sentence or the firing-squad?

The man on the floor continued to regard Landon with his brilliant black eyes. He had moved a little closer to the wall so that he could rest his head against it as he smoked.

"I think, señor, that I have seen you before."

"I don't think so," Landon said.

The rags stirred slightly, as though the man were shrugging his shoulders where he lay.

"Perhaps not. It is of no importance."

"As you say, it is of no importance."

"And yet I should have said that I had seen you with Pedro Gonzales."

"You are mistaken. I know no Pedro Gonzales," Landon said harshly.

4

"Then of course I am mistaken. No matter. The señor is Americano?"

"No; English."

"Ah; and no doubt the señor comes to Santa Ana for holiday — for pleasure perhaps?"

The heaps of rags shook with subdued laughter. Landon did not share the joke; he stared bleakly at the opposite wall and made no answer. The man on the floor watched him through a thin haze of smoke, perhaps trying to weigh up this fair-haired, stocky Englishman, with the broad shoulders and bony face, cold blue eyes, and mouth that was like the gash of a knife. Cruel? Perhaps. Ruthless? Most probably. Used to giving orders? Without doubt.

"Life is hard, señor." The man on the floor sighed gustily. "One day we are free men; the next we are in gaol, shut in by four walls and a barred door. Life is very hard."

Landon did not answer. The man continued to puff at his cigarette. When he had finished it he stretched, yawned, gathered his rags about him, and went to sleep.

5

Landon remained standing. There was nothing to sit on except the floor, and that, having so obviously been used for the relief of nature, did not attract him. He made a movement as though to look at his wrist-watch, but then remembered that the police had taken it. It was a good Swiss watch — self-winding, waterproof, the most valuable thing he possessed; it had accompanied him through the War, been with him in good fortune and in bad; it was like a friend, and he would be sorry to lose it. He supposed the chances of getting it back were slender.

About an hour later the key grated once again in the lock, and the prison door swung open. The policeman who had shut Landon in stood in the doorway.

"Captain Garcia is ready to interrogate you. You will come with me."

They walked down a short corridor and into a large, untidy room littered with official-looking files, ledgers, and loose papers. Behind a desk, seated in a swivel chair and facing the door, was a short, stout, bald-headed man with a thin white scar crossing his forehead horizontally and passing back behind each ear, as though at some time in the past some one had been stopped in the act of scalping him. A series of heavy chins folding over the collar of a khaki tunic were black, with the sproutings of a new beard, although it was evident from traces of lather under the left ear that he had shaved quite recently. Behind him was a large window opening on to a kind of courtyard enclosed by the buildings of the police-station. The light threw a fat shadow of Captain Garcia on to the desk in front of him.

"Your name is Landon — Harvey Landon. Is that correct?"

"Yes."

Landon saw that lying on the desk were the personal belongings that the police had taken from him — his watch, his wallet, a few coins, a ball-point pen, a pocket-knife, his passport. He wondered why they had left him his cigarettes; perhaps they were not altogether inhuman, or perhaps it was merely carelessness.

Captain Garcia leaned back in his chair and crossed one short, plump leg over the other. He did not invite Landon to sit down. His voice was soft; it seemed to escape from the thick, rather moist lips like a little rush of steam, without any assistance from the man himself.

"I should like to know why you came to the Central Republic. You will tell me, please."

"I came because I wished to."

"Naturally. I did not suppose that you had been forced to come." Garcia's eyes peered sleepily at Landon from puffy eyelids. He looked as if he had spent a sleepless night, perhaps many sleepless nights. He gave the impression of performing a wearisome task with weary resignation. "But there was possibly some purpose behind your visit? You did not come simply for pleasure?"

"What makes you suppose that?"

"Señor Landon, you are not, I think, a very rich man."

Landon's mouth tightened. This policeman appeared to know something about him. No, he was certainly not a rich man. Since leaving the Royal Navy he had at times been very poor indeed.

Garcia leaned forward and shuffled

some papers on the desk. He picked one up.

"You arrived in Rio de Janiero on the twenty-second of July. That is so?"

There was no point in denying the fact; it had been reported in the Brazilian newspapers. Landon had sailed into Rio harbour in an eight-ton yawl, having completed the voyage from Plymouth single-handed, touching at Madeira and the Cape Verde Islands *en route*. He had arrived in Rio with a few clothes, a yawl, and no money. He had had to sell the yawl in order to eat.

Garcia went on reading, glancing now and then at Landon with his heavy-lidded eyes.

"In Rio you made contact with Don Diego Vargas."

So they knew that too. It was true, of course. Landon had been in Rio no more than a week, living on the proceeds of the sale of his boat, when Diego flew in. He had heard of Landon's arrival and wanted to see him, partly for the sake of old times when they had been friends at Oxford, partly for another reason.

"You know Don Diego well?" Garcia asked.

"Well enough."

"He is a dangerous man. Perhaps it is unwise to associate with such men — for one's own safety, you understand."

Landon knew what Garcia meant: it had to do with the second reason for Diego's wish to renew an old acquaintance. Diego and others of a similar political persuasion were planning a coup; they could use men like Landon, men with knowledge of guns, ammunition, drill. And Landon was not without experience of revolutions. He had been mixed up in similar troubles in Central America. Diego seemed to know all about that; he knew also that Landon could speak Spanish.

"This employment may amuse you."

Landon was more interested in the rate of pay than in the amusing nature of the job. Don Diego assured him that he would be suitably rewarded.

"And it will give me so much pleasure, Harvey, to have you with me. It will be like old times."

Landon remembered those old times;

10

there had been some hectic escapades, and both of them had been lucky to avoid serious consequences. They had been very young then, and wild. Diego, dark and handsome in an almost sinister way, had been a great ladies' man. Now he was almost twice as old, austere-looking, his black hair tinged with grey, his face thin and hollow-cheeked, with a straight, thin nose and delicately pointed chin.

In the Central Republic he was a man of substance — he owned estates totalling many thousands of acres — but he did not see eye to eye with the government of General Romero. Diego was a liberal, violently opposed to the near-dictatorship of Romero and the oppressive measures enforced by a police system modelled on the pre-war German model, and even trained by ex-Nazis.

The politics of the affair did not interest Landon greatly; apart from the friendship that he still felt for Don Diego, his reasons for allying himself with the revolutionary cause were entirely mercenary. He made no secret of the fact.

"That is understood," Diego said. "But

you can help us none the less for that. We have the enthusiasm already. What we need is the skill and experience."

Landon willingly traded his knowledge of the arts of war for their money. In secret mountain strongholds he drilled patriots in the use of small arms, twenty-millimetre cannon, and light artillery. He found his employers generous, and until this moment had no cause to regret his acceptance of Diego's offer.

"The government of the Central Republic," Garcia said softly, "is not blind and it is not deaf. Neither is it composed of idiots. It knows more of what goes on in some parts of the country than certain people suppose. It has its spies, its informers. You have been unwise to meddle in matters that do not concern you. Now I fear you will have to suffer the consequences of your foolishness. Unless — "

"Unless?"

Captain Garcia pulled at his rubbery lower lip. "If you are co-operative things may not be too bad for you." He picked up Landon's watch, held it to his ear for a moment, and put it back on the desk. "You might even suffer no inconvenience whatever as a result of your illegal activities in this country."

"Of what am I accused?" Landon asked.

Garcia permitted himself a fleeting smile. "Señor Landon, do not let us waste time on questions of purely academic interest. Let us concern ourselves only with important matters. I have said that you can avoid all unpleasant consequences of your activities if you agree to certain conditions."

"And those are?"

"Very simple, very simple indeed." Captain Garcia uncrossed his legs, took a pen from the row clipped into his breast pocket, drew a blank pad towards him, leaned his elbows on the desk, and prepared to write. "You will answer the questions I put to you fully and truthfully." His voice had sharpened suddenly; the appearance of lethargy had left him. He looked ruthless, efficient, the white band of the scar ringing his head like a cord.

"I will answer nothing," Landon said.

Garcia's eyes became narrow slits. "I

13

think you will answer — if not now, then later. It would be better if you answered now — better for you, better for me. It would avoid much unpleasantness. First, then, what was your purpose in coming into Santa Ana?"

"I wished to buy a shirt."

He saw the disbelief in Garcia's face, yet in part at least the answer was true; he had wanted to buy a shirt. That he had also been conveying a message from Don Diego to a certain Rodriguez Pancorbo was something that he did not choose to reveal. The message had been verbal; it was locked in his own mind; no one could discover it against his will.

"Santa Ana is safe for you," Don Diego had said. "Pedro will go with you; he is unknown there also. You will both be quite safe."

Yet some one must have recognized them as they rode in; some one must have betrayed them to the police. Garcia had mentioned spies, informers; and it was impossible to organize a revolution without taking into the ranks some doubtful recruits. Landon would have liked to know who had warned the

14

police, who had put the finger on him. He thought suddenly of the heap of rags, the man to whom he had given a cigarette; that man had said: 'You were riding with Pedro Gonzales.' Then he must obviously have known Pedro. Could he have been the spy? And if so, why was he also in prison?

There was one consolation — Pedro had got away. He would warn Don Diego. If the police knew so much it was no longer wise for Diego to remain in this part of the country.

"You brought a message to some one," Garcia said. "I want the name of that man."

So they did not know everything. They had some information but they wanted more. Well, they would get none from him.

"I had no message. I came to buy a shirt."

"And where is this shirt? Will you show it to me?"

"I did not buy it. I had no time. I was arrested."

Garcia spread out his hands on the desk, palms downward. The fingers were

15

short and thick, with black hairs sprouting from them. The nails were surprisingly well manicured.

"Why do you not admit that there was no question of buying shirts?" He spoke gently again, as though reasoning with a refractory child. "Why not admit that you were bringing a message? Really, it is for your own good that I beg you to be reasonable. It is not fitting that a man like you, Señor Landon, should lie in gaol with the scum and filth of Santa Ana. Do you not agree?"

Landon did not hesitate to agree wholeheartedly with this admirable sentiment, and Garcia seemed to take this measure of agreement as a good sign. He pulled the pad once more towards him and picked up his pen. He showed an almost boyish eagerness to write.

"There might even be a reward," he murmured. "I promise nothing, of course, but a certain value is placed on information of the right kind. Now let us get down to business." It was as though he realized that the formal preliminaries of refusing to answer, of professing innocence, had to be gone

16

through, but that now that they had been completed nothing further lay in the path of a complete and truthful answer to all questions. "Now then, the name of the man to whom you were taking the message."

His reaction to Landon's continued and stubborn refusal to answer was first one of surprise, then of pain, finally of anger. He pounded on the desk with his fists, making the watch and coins dance up and down. "You shall answer! By God, but you shall answer! I have no more time to waste on you now, but I warn you, there are ways of making obstinate tongues wag. Think it over, Señor Landon; think it over and be wise."

He turned to the policeman, who all the while had been lounging against the doorpost. "Take the prisoner away. Take him out of my sight."

The heap of rags stirred when Landon was thrust once again into the prison room, the black eyes opened, the mouth yawned.

"Another cigarette, I beg, señor."

Landon flung the man a cigarette

and a match. The match scraped on the wall of the room, spluttered into flame. The man moved himself, drew up his legs, and squatted on his haunches, letting smoke drift around his beaked nose.

"A wretched life, señor. Under a different government it would all be different." He gazed at Landon, his eyes suddenly sharp, intelligent. "We understand each other, eh?"

Landon said: "Who are you?" Now that he looked at the man more closely he had an idea that he had seen him before. But where?

"My name is Miguel Gomez, at your service." Still squatting on his haunches, he made a mock bow.

"What service can you do me?"

"In this unfortunate situation — none. We are brothers in misfortune. We might have been brothers in good fortune. But no matter."

"What do you mean by that?"

Miguel Gomez closed one eye. "If certain changes were to occur in this country — we will not say what changes — you and I, señor, would be on the

18

same side. You understand?"

Landon said nothing. Miguel drew in a long breath of smoke and allowed it to come puffing up with his words, as though he were a steam-engine gathering speed.

"These swine have questioned you." He made a motion of his hand to indicate that he was referring to the police. "What have you told them?"

"Nothing. I have nothing to tell." Landon was wary.

"Nothing to tell. No, of course not. Nothing." Miguel gazed at the end of his cigarette. "Nothing for them, of course. But for a certain personage there was perhaps a — message. That message has not perhaps been delivered. And you are likely to be here a long time, señor. It is a great misfortune." He paused, then continued slowly, choosing his words with care: "I, on the other hand, will be released to-day; that is certain." He looked up at Landon, his eyes glittering. "I could take that message for you."

Landon bent down and grasped the rags covering Miguel's chest, heaving him to his feet. He remembered now where he had seen the man. That face — hawk-like, villainous — it had been in the crowd when he had been arrested; it had been close to one of the police. There could be no doubt now; this was the traitor — this stool-pigeon, now planted here to extract from him by guile the information that Garcia had failed to get by direct questioning and the offer of a bribe.

"Damned swine!" He banged Miguel's head against the wall. "Damned, filthy, rotten swine!"

Miguel wrenched himself free and ran to the door. He grasped the bars and shook them violently, yelling. The gaoler came running.

"What is it? Confound you, why all this noise?"

"Let me out," Miguel cried. "Let me out before this madman kills me."

The gaoler unlocked the door and opened it, grumbling: "I said it would be no good. All along I said so. He is no fool, that one. Come out, then, if you want to."

Miguel slipped through the gap that

20

had been opened for him. The door clanged shut again, and the key turned in the lock.

Landon took another cigarette and scraped a match on the wall.

# 2

## The Commission

AT mid-day a meal was brought to him — a kind of stew in an earthenware bowl, a hunk of coarse bread, and a mug of water. When the bowl and mug had been taken away he began to pace restlessly back and forth across the room, trying to think of a way to regain his freedom.

An active man, he felt all the more irked by the confinement of four walls. He had been used to the wide view — the rolling wastes of the sea or, more recently, the pampas and the mountains — now his vision was restricted to a white-washed room, an iron door, and two barred windows set so high in the wall that it was impossible to see out of them. Through the windows came daylight and the voices of free men, so tantalizingly close that he felt like shouting to them; but he did not do so, knowing that it would be useless to call to them for aid. He kicked viciously at the floor, and a little spurt of dust rose into the air. He looked at the windows, gauging the strength of the bars; they were an inch in diameter, set firmly in the brickwork. There was no hope there.

By evening he had acquired companions. One by one they were bundled into the room, the door clanging shut behind them. They were what Captain Garcia had so accurately described as the scum and filth of Santa Ana — drunken half-breeds, thieves, vagabonds, evil in appearance and odour. Landon retired to a corner and stared morosely at the floor.

He was roused from his meditations by a hoarse voice whispering in his ear: "Courage, señor. Do not despair. Help will come."

He looked in surprise at the man who had crept up beside him. Beneath the dirt he saw a face that he knew, one that he would surely have recognized when the man was pushed into the room if he had not been wrapped up in his own thoughts, oblivious of what

23

went on around him.

"Juan!"

The man put a finger to his lips warningly. He was one of Don Diego's men. Landon had taught him the working of a Browning machine-gun; he had been an apt pupil.

He whispered again, not looking at Landon, seemingly uninterested in the Englishman: "All is arranged. To-night we shall be free. Keep away from the outer wall."

He drew a pouch of tobacco from his pocket and began to roll a cigarette, singing softly to himself. Landon's spirits rose, cheered by the presence of Juan and the news that friends outside the gaol were active on his behalf. In moments of doubt he had thought that perhaps they would leave him to his fate. Now he felt ashamed of having entertained such suspicions; he ought to have known Don Diego better.

Juan whispered through the smoke of his cigarette: "At two in the morning, when the town is asleep, we shall be out of this sty."

"I shall not be sorry," Landon muttered.

"No." Juan moved away to another part of the room and squatted down on his haunches. In one corner a drunk was relieving himself without shame. Landon's legs were aching; he scraped a small space of floor near one wall with the sole of his boot and sat down with his back resting against the wall.

The extra bodies in the room made the heat and the stench almost overpowering. Landon took out his packet of cigarettes and found that there were eight left. He reckoned that the time must now be about eight o'clock, and Juan had said that they would be released at two o'clock in the morning — by what means he had not explained. That meant another six hours to wait; he would have to ration his smoking. He wished he had his watch; it angered him to think that he would be forced to leave it behind, and he could imagine it finding its way to the fat wrist of Captain Garcia.

He began to doze, his head lolling forward upon his knees, his body relaxed.

He awoke to find that the daylight had faded and the room had become cooler. Around him he could hear men snoring, breathing heavily in their sleep. He felt Juan's hand on his arm.

"It draws close to the time, señor."

Landon could see a glimmer of white where the two windows were situated. A pale suggestion of moonlight filtered into the room.

"I must put out the marker," Juan whispered.

"Marker?"

"This." He held out his hand, and Landon saw what appeared to be a length of string with a small metal ring tied to each end. Juan moved to the outer wall, stepping carefully over the sleeping prisoners. With a curving movement of his arm he flung one ring towards one of the windows; it clinked faintly against a bar and fell on the outside of the building, taking one end of the string with it. The other ring was still in Juan's hand; he dropped it against the wall, so that now the string hung over the sill of the barred window, marking the position of the room.

"Now there will be no mistake," he said.

Landon took out his packet of cigarettes

26

again. He had slept away five hours, and there were still eight cigarettes left. He could afford to be generous; he offered them to Juan, and the man took one with a muttered word of thanks. The splutter of the match sounded startlingly loud, but the prisoners were sound sleepers, and they did not stir. Juan and Landon crouched side by side, smoking, shielding the glow of their cigarettes with cupped hands.

"How will they do it?" Landon asked.

He could see Juan's dark face turned towards him in the gloom. "That we shall see. I only know that we must keep away from the outer wall."

"Why?"

"It may be dangerous."

"There are two men sleeping beside it. What of them?"

"They must take their chance. It would raise the alarm if we tried to move them. We cannot bother our heads with the fate of such as those."

The time passed slowly. They smoked the rest of Landon's cigarettes and two that Juan rolled. They heard faint sounds outside the prison. Then the string twitched. Landon did not notice it, but Juan had keen eyes.

"It is the signal."

He crossed the room softly and gave an answering tug on the string. Then he came back and crouched down beside Landon.

"Best to lie down now, señor, with our backs to the room."

Landon thought of the state of the floor, but did as Juan suggested. Ten minutes passed. He heard a sound like a rat gnawing. Then the sound stopped. Another minute wore slowly away, and suddenly the outer wall exploded in a mass of dust and rubble. A red glow like a ball of fire illuminated the room for a moment and then died. A piece of brick struck Landon's shoulder with a numbing blow, and mortar dust choked his throat. Juan was pulling at his sleeve, his voice urgent: "Come quickly now, quickly!"

Landon heard a man screaming and frightened voices. The dust seemed to be everywhere, clogging his nostrils, leaving a coating on his tongue; it mingled with the pungent odour of explosives. In the outer wall a jagged hole had opened.

28

Beside the hole a man lay in a contorted heap; it was from this heap that the screams were coming. They ended in a sudden throaty gurgle, as if the man were being choked by a flow of blood.

All the prisoners seemed to be shouting at the tops of their voices, and the room was a confused mass of bodies. At any moment the police would arrive to see what all the noise was about. There was no time to spare.

"Quick!" Juan cried again. He pushed Landon towards the hole outlined by the moonlight. Landon tripped over a dark body, felt a hand convulsively grasp his ankle, kicked violently with the other foot at something soft and yielding, and felt the hand relax its grip. He ducked through the hole and found himself outside the gaol in one of the back streets of Santa Ana.

There were men and horses; they seemed to block the narrow way. A voice — it was Don Diego's — said calmly, cutting thought the confusion: "Into the saddle! Hurry!"

Landon found himself being lifted on to the back of one of the horses, his feet thrust into the stirrups, reins pushed into his hands. Then the whole band of horsemen was on the move through the sleeping streets of Santa Ana, and the entire operation had taken no more than a few brief, incidental-packed minutes. They left behind them a breached wall, a dying man, five confused prisoners who did not know whether to stay or to make use of this opportunity to escape, and a number of policemen so bemused with sleep and confusion that by the time they had found out what had happened and had decided what to do about it Don Diego and his party were clear of the town and riding over open country away into the night.

Don Diego moved his horse close to Landon's. "You are all right, Harvey, my friend?"

"I'm all right, but I believe you killed one poor devil. You made a big explosion."

"It could not be helped. We had to be certain the charge was big enough to break open the wall. Too small a charge would have ruined everything. But you were not hurt?"

30

"A piece of brick hit my shoulder. It is nothing — stiffness; a bruise perhaps. It will soon go."

"We will look at it later."

"Where are we going? The old place will not be safe now. Garcia knows that I have been working for you."

"Does he know about the message — about Rodriguez?"

"He seemed to know, or to guess, there was a message, but I gave him no information. I don't think he knows about Rodriguez. In fact, I feel sure he doesn't."

"Good, good. Plans will have to be altered, that is all. Romero is waking up. We must proceed with care. He has his spies everywhere."

"There was one in prison with me — Miguel Gomez. It was he, I think, who gave me away to Garcia's men."

"Gomez, eh? So he has turned traitor. Bah, it matters little; he does not know much; he was of no great importance to the cause. However I shall remember."

Don Diego was silent for a while. The horsemen were no longer in one group but spread out along the trail.

31

The moon was dropping low in the sky, but there were no clouds, and the stars were brightening as the moon waned. They had slackened their pace now, saving the horses for a long ride. Hoofs beat dully on the ground, bridles jingled faintly. There was no indication of pursuit. They had come into Santa Ana like ghosts, and like ghosts they had faded into the night.

Don Diego suddenly remembered the question that Landon had asked. He said: "No, we are not going to the old place. As you say, it would not be safe now. That is where Garcia will search, but he will find nothing. For the present it will be necessary to withdraw to the mountains; but for you I have other plans."

"What plans?"

"That you shall hear when we reach our destination, the place where we are to rest."

Dawn was breaking when they reached the place that Diego had spoken about; a grey light spreading up from the east and creeping over the pampas revealed a plain log-house in all its stark simplicity.

32

They dismounted.

"We breakfast here," Diego said. "Then we move on. It will not be safe to stay here for long; it is too close to Santa Ana and our fine friend, Garcia."

The horses were led away by some of the men to be fed and watered while the others went into the cabin.

Diego gave curt orders: "Carlos, Adolfo — prepare the breakfast. Come, Harvey, we have something to talk over; and you, Pedro, come also. There is little time to waste."

He drew Landon and Gonzales into an inner room roughly partitioned off from the large communal bunk-room of the gaucho cabin. In it was a table and some chairs. They sat down, Landon facing Don Diego across the table, Gonzales on one side, like a referee between them.

"Events have moved faster than we anticipated," Diego said. "As I told you, we have had to alter our plans — drastically. You, Harvey, must leave the country."

"Leave?"

Diego nodded. In the gradually

strengthening light his face looked grey and lined, as though he were troubled, as though problems were pressing hard upon him.

"We have a task for you, a most important task, one that I would entrust only to a man in whom I had complete faith. On the successful completion of this task depends to a large extent the success or failure of our great purpose."

He felt in the pocket of his jacket and drew out a sealed envelope. He laid the envelope on the table between himself and Landon, tapping it gently with his long, slender forefinger.

"You are to deliver this to a Mr Delgado in New York." He took a slip of paper from his pocket and wrote on it with rapid, nervous strokes of a pen. "There, that is the address. You will memorize it and then destroy the paper. The address is not written on the letter for reasons of security. You understand?"

"I understand," Landon said. He was glancing at the address on the slip of paper. He knew the district; it was somewhere along the skyscrapers at the

34

southern end of Manhattan Island. It seemed a long, long way from a loghouse on the pampas of South America.

Don Diego continued, his eyes holding Landon's: "You will hand the letter to Mr Delgado himself. If for any reason you are unable to contact Mr Delgado you are to destroy the letter without opening it; you are to give it to no one else. I think I need not stress the importance of preventing the letter from falling into the hands of our enemies; that would be a disaster."

He paused a moment, keeping his gaze fixed unwaveringly on Landon, as though trying to assess his reactions to this commission. Then he went on.

"When you have delivered the letter your work for us is finished. It will not be safe for you ever to return to this country — not, that is, until the revolution has been successful. That success depends to a very great extent on you. It is Delgado who arranges certain affairs for us; there is a question of aircraft; we cannot succeed without planes. I will not say more; the less you know the better if certain unpleasant things should happen. This letter will tell Delgado what to do."

Diego was silent for a few minutes, drumming on the table with the tips of his fingers. Then he said: "You may be wondering why we do not send the letter by some other means. Unfortunately, the normal methods are barred to us; the post is examined. It is known that Delgado is our agent, and to put such a letter as this into the post would be equivalent to presenting it to Romero. No, it must be carried by some one we can trust, some one resourceful, some one who is not afraid of danger."

"You think I fit that specification?"

"If I were not certain of it," Diego said, "I should not be handing you this letter."

Landon glanced at the envelope; it was buff-coloured, plain, with a red blob of sealing-wax on the flap and the imprint of Don Diego's signet-ring. He was thinking, debating in his mind how this assignment would be likely to affect his future. He would not be sorry to leave the Central Republic; he was ready for a change. Having carried out this task, he would be free to go off on some other tack. Maybe he would find something of interest in the United States; he might be able to pick up another boat, cruise down to the West Indies, and sail westward through the Panama Canal and across the Pacific. His pulse quickened at the thought. But he would need money.

As if he had read Landon's mind, Diego said: "When you have delivered the letter Delgado will pay you five thousand American dollars; the letter authorizes him to do so. This is partly the arrears of your pay which has accumulated while you have worked for us and partly a bonus for your task as courier. I think you will agree that it is to your advantage to receive payment in dollars; they are so much more negotiable than other currency."

Landon grinned. "It also provides a strong incentive for me to get the letter safely to its destination."

A smile flickered across Diego's lean, hollow-cheeked face. "We would have trusted you anyway, but, as you say, five thousand dollars are an incentive."

"It is very generous," Landon said. It

was much more than he had expected. With that amount he would be stepping off on the right foot in New York. He would certainly contact Mr Delgado.

"You are prepared to undertake this commission?" Don Diego asked.

"I most certainly am."

"Good. Now to details. You must realize that the task will not be without its dangers. In the first place you have to cross the border. You are known to Garcia, your description will have been circulated, and frontier posts will be on the look-out for an Englishman with fair hair, pale blue eyes and thin lips. Even when you have managed to get across the border you will still be in danger; the Central Republic has its agents in Argentina."

"Once in Argentina," Landon said, "they'll have a job to catch me. The problem will be to get over the border."

"Exactly." Don Diego got up from his chair, went to an old-fashioned roll-top desk, and found a map of South America. He brought it to the table and stabbed his finger at the vein-like marking of a railway. "That is the way you will travel as far as Almagro. There you will have to leave the train. You cannot show your passport, and I am afraid we have not the time to obtain a false one."

"I no longer have my own, anyway," Landon said. "Garcia took it."

Don Diego looked concerned. "That may be awkward for you when it comes to getting away from Argentina."

"I'll manage," Landon said. "But how do I get across the border?"

"That, I am afraid, will have to be left to your own resourcefulness. If you do not think you are able to do it say so at once. I could find another agent, though perhaps not one in whom I was willing to put so much trust."

Pedro said suddenly, cutting into the exchanges for the first time: "If Señor Landon is afraid I am ready to go. It is a pity that I cannot speak English, but no matter."

Landon said sharply: "I am not afraid. I will find a way of getting across the border; you need have no fear of that." He picked up the sealed envelope and thrust it into an inner pocket of his jacket. "And I will contact Mr Delgado; you may set your mind at rest about that also."

Pedro's brown, rugged face creased into a grin. "I did not doubt you. I spoke only to fire your blood. Yes, most surely you will find Delgado."

Don Diego straightened his back. "Good. Then that is settled. And now perhaps a wash and shave." He glanced at the spiky stubble on Landon's face and smiled. "Then breakfast, and away. Sleep, I am afraid, must wait."

"I'll sleep in the train," Landon said.

# 3

## Rail and Road

IF Landon had not been so thoroughly worn out he would never have found it possible to sleep in the railway truck. He was lying on a bed of sacks, with a tarpaulin above him. The tarpaulin was supported by an iron bar running the length of the truck, and between the sacks and the bar was a narrow space into which Landon had been able to squeeze. He wondered what was in the sacks; it felt like something hard and knobbly, not by any means the ideal material for a bed. But Landon was exhausted, and though he tried to keep awake until the train started, he was already sleeping soundly when the truck jerked forward and rolled off into the night.

When Don Diego had mentioned that he would have to travel to the border by train Landon had imagined a passenger train. Diego had quickly disillusioned

41

him. "It would be madness. The police will be checking all passengers; you could not hope to slip through. No; I have a better plan. There is a freight train that halts at Lucena to allow a passenger train to go through. That will be your transport."

It had been easy to board the freight train at Lucena, a small wayside station on the edge of the Vargas estate. They had ridden for most of the day, and it was again night when they arrived at the station. The train was, as Don Diego had said, shunted away in a siding, dark and silent.

"The crew go off for refreshment at this halt," Diego explained. "I know all this because it is my business to know such things. This will not be the first time that I have made use of this train."

Pedro loosened the tarpaulin and helped Landon into the truck that they had chosen; it was close to the middle of the train.

"Good-bye, Harvey, my friend, and good fortune," Don Diego said. "Some day in happier circumstances we may meet again."

"What do you intend to do?" Landon asked. "The hunt will be on for you as well."

"I shall soon be in a safe place," Diego said. "There is no need to worry about me."

Landon knew what he meant; he would retire to one of those mountain strongholds where the revolutionaries were concentrated. From there an army could not have winkled them out. There they would wait until Delgado had received the letter and the time was ripe to strike.

"Good-bye, then," Landon said. "And may all go well with you."

It was the rain that woke Landon, rain dripping through a hole in the tarpaulin and falling on his face. He shifted his position, moving away from the drops of water, and felt the cold under-surface of the tarpaulin rubbing on his neck. The truck was shaking and rattling, and he could hear the clatter of the wheels and the splattering of rain. He wondered how long he had slept, and again he felt the loss of his watch. He had no means of telling how far the train had travelled.

He wormed his way to the rear end of the truck where Pedro had loosened the tarpaulin, lifted it, and peered out. Complete darkness met his gaze, darkness and a flurry of rain. He dropped the flap and moved back towards the centre of the truck.

Diego had told him that the train would reach the border town of Almagro early in the morning, and he would then have to slip out of his hiding-place and try to get away unobserved. If any railwaymen saw him it would probably be easy to bribe them into blindness with a handful of money. Diego had provided Landon with ample cash to meet any such eventuality. But it would be safer to get away unseen.

The train rattled on its way, the wheels hammering at the joints in the rails, the tarpaulin drumming under the raindrops. All these sounds, which might have been calculated to keep Landon awake, induced instead an overwhelming sleepiness in his still-tired body. He found a dry place on the sacks and in a moment was again sound asleep.

He awoke a second time to the

44

realization that the train and also the rain had stopped. It was probably the sudden ceasing of the rattle and vibration of the truck that had aroused him. Faintly he could hear a hiss of steam escaping from the engine, and, faintly too, a man's voice somewhere in the distance, singing.

He wriggled to the back of the truck and lifted the tarpaulin cautiously. Some water that had collected in a hollow of the sheet splashed down on to the buffers and the linkage with a noise that to Landon seemed to drown all else with its thunder. He peered over the edge of the truck and saw that dawn was close at hand. The trucks behind the one in which he had travelled through the night stretched away like so many shadows, becoming less and less clear as the distance widened. On either side of the train appeared to be open ground, fading into darkness; it was impossible to see clearly for more than a few yards.

Landon wondered whether the train had been held up on the outskirts of Almagro. If so, nothing could be better suited to his purpose of getting clear without being seen. He decided to get out of the truck and see whether there was anything to indicate the presence of a town not far away.

Some water ran down his neck as he crawled from under the tarpaulin and down on to the rear buffers of the truck. He jumped from the buffers and landed in soft, damp grass at the side of the truck. The grass was long enough to give him some cover, and he felt sure that if he lay flat he would not be seen from either the engine or the guard's van. He raised his head cautiously and looked, as he supposed, in the direction of Almagro. But the train was on a curve and blocked his view, and in order to widen the angle he began to crawl through the grass away from the track.

When he had put about twenty yards between himself and the train he raised his head again. In the distance beyond the engine he could see a red signal light, and beyond that a few other lights and a dark huddle outlined against the sky that might have been the buildings of a station.

Landon felt sure after a few moments that this could not be Almagro or even

46

the outskirts of that town. There were no other lights beyond the station that would suggest a populous town waking up to a new day; and the station itself, if such in fact it was, seemed to be small and unimportant. It might well be that many miles still separated him from his destination of Almagro, and he decided to reboard the train.

He had just come to this decision when the engine gave a brief toot on its whistle, gasped like a man emptying his lungs, and began to move, clankingly, slowly at first, then gradually gathering speed.

Landon jumped to his feet and began running towards it on an oblique line, trying to catch up with the truck in which he had travelled. The train was on a down slope, and its speed increased rapidly. Landon made a last effort to draw level with his truck, tripped over some obstacle lying beside the track, and fell flat on his face. He heard the wheels of the train clanking and banging past him, and rolled himself away from them, fearing that some projecting bar or chain might strike him. A moment later he saw the van go swaying past, and caught a glimpse of the guard's astonished face as he gazed down at this man lying beside the track.

Then the red light of the van was receding into the grey dusk of early morning, and Landon was standing up and brushing the dirt from his clothes with his bare hands. His first thought was for the letter; he felt in his pocket to make sure that it had not been lost and was reassured by the feel of the crisp, sealed envelope. Mr Delgado was still a long way off, but he would receive his letter.

Meanwhile the first problem was to get to Almagro. At least he knew what direction to take; he had simply to follow the train. He stepped on to the track and began to walk towards the glimmer of lights in the distance.

As he drew nearer Landon became further convinced that this could be no outlying part of Almagro. The train had gone straight through, and the huddle of buildings was no more than a huddle — a signal-box, a few offices, a galvanized-iron shed. On arrival at the station he saw a board bearing in white-painted letters the name Cabildo, and he tried to see again in his mind's eye Don Diego's map. Cabildo — surely there was a town or village of that name some thirty kilometres out of Almagro? If so he had a long walk in front of him.

He was still looking at the signboard when a man came out of one of the offices and gazed at him with an air of astonishment and mistrust.

"What do you want? Where have you come from?"

He was dressed in a kind of semi-uniform, rather worn and tattered. He wore the peaked cap and brass-buttoned coat of the railway, but the lower half of him was clothed in patched, baggy trousers of the type that the peons wore. He was a small, bowed man with a face like a weasel and black, drooping moustaches.

"I want to reach Almagro," Landon said.

"It is four hours to the next train."

The man was carrying a signal-lamp in his hand. He raised it, shining the light on Landon's face, as if to see more clearly what manner of customer it was with whom he had to deal. What he saw did not appear to reassure him. "Where have you come from?"

In mentioning his wish to get to Almagro Landon had said the first thing that came into his head. Obviously this railwayman thought he wanted to go by train, but that was impossible. Still avoiding a direct answer to the question as to where he had come from, Landon asked whether there was any possibility of obtaining breakfast, for he was feeling hungry. The weasel-faced man jerked a thumb over his shoulder in a vague indication of direction.

"At the Hotel Alameda perhaps."

"Where is that?"

The man seemed about to ask again where Landon had come from. He had perhaps a right to be suspicious when a perfect stranger suddenly appeared at daybreak, apparently from nowhere, just as though he had descended on the station by parachute. Indeed, he did glance into the sky, as if that explanation had occurred to him. But after a little hesitation he said gruffly: "Come; I will show you."

He turned and led the way out of the station; then he pointed to a road full of potholes, puddled by the night's rain. The light had rapidly strengthened, and Landon could see a long, wide street of houses which he supposed must be the town of Cabildo.

"It's on the right; the first building. Hotel Alameda. But you're probably too early."

He seemed to be wondering whether to make one last attempt to discover where Landon had come from, but thought better of it, shrugged his shoulders, and went back to the station. Landon walked down the deserted road towards the Hotel Alameda.

The houses of Cabildo would not have delighted the eye of an architect with any feeling for his craft. They were, for the most part, miserable shacks, exhibiting no signs of prosperity. In fact, it seemed to Landon strange that a town so obviously poor should have been able to boast a hotel at all. But the Alameda, as he soon discovered, was in keeping with the rest of the place. It was a wooden building, one storey high, with a roof of rusty corrugated iron. In front of it a few bedraggled chickens scratched in the mud, and at one side a goat tethered to a stake munched stolidly away at some rank-looking herbage. The front door of the hotel stood open, and Landon walked straight in.

The room in which he immediately found himself was sparsely furnished with a bare wooden table and a few plain chairs. There was no one in it, so Landon pushed his way through to another room at the back. This appeared to be the kitchen, and he discovered an old Indian woman stooping over a cooking-stove. Her dress was black, and she had black hair hanging down on either side of her face like the mane of a horse. The face itself was almost unbelievably wrinkled; in colour and texture it was like an old, cracked leather shoe. She might have passed, without any make-up, for one of the witches in *Macbeth*.

She straightened up as much as her permanently crooked back would allow when Landon stepped into the room and drew away fearfully, gripping a ladle in one hand, as though for defence. Her voice quavered.

"Who are you? What do you want?"

"I am a traveller and I want breakfast," Landon said.

She seemed only slightly reassured by his words. She continued to back away from him until the wall halted her.

"It is too early." She held up three fingers like old dried chicken-bones. "Three hours before breakfast."

"I want it now."

"It is not possible. You must wait. It is too early."

Landon said quietly: "It could be managed. Anything will do — bread and cold meat, a bottle of wine, anything. But I must have it now. He felt in his pocket and pulled out some paper money. He handed it to the old woman; she took it, examined it, and thrust it away inside her dress.

"Very well. I find you something. You eat it in here, then go."

There was a crafty look on her face, and Landon guessed that she wanted to get him away quickly before anyone else was up, so that she could keep the money for herself. He did not mind; he could have asked for nothing better. The sooner he was out of this town and on his way to Almagro the safer he would feel.

The breakfast turned out far better than he had expected. The old woman prepared an omelette and made coffee. She did not give him wine — perhaps that would have had to be accounted for — but he preferred the coffee. He ate quickly, eager to go; and the woman watched him without curiosity, apparently feeling no interest in his identity, no wish to know how he had come to the hotel, eager only to be rid of him so that she could keep to herself the money that he had paid.

Landon asked her: "Which is the road to Almagro?"

She grinned, showing the filthy brown stumps of her teeth, hanging like so many rotting stakes from the sockets of her gums. "There is only one road, señor. You go through the town, straight on. It will take you to Almagro."

"How far?"

"Twenty-five kilometres — thirty perhaps." It was obvious that she did not know the exact distance and did not care. What was distance? She would never travel that road again.

Landon finished his omelette and asked for another cup of coffee. The woman poured it, grumbling softly: "You must hurry. I have work to do." She was eager to be rid of him.

Landon sipped the coffee, and his eye was caught by a newspaper lying on the floor. He picked it up and noted with rising interest that it was dated the previous day. He smoothed it out and saw almost immediately, staring at him from the front page, the words: 'Santa Ana Gaol Break. Man Killed. Two Injured. Search for Englishman.'

So they were really on the hunt for him. He had known it already, but seeing it in print seemed to bring it home to him more forcibly, to make it real. He read quickly through the account, the old woman fussing impatiently with a broom around the table. It told him little that was news to him. A notorious foreign revolutionary who had entered the country with the express purpose of overthrowing the benevolent government of General Romero had been arrested in Santa Ana by Captain Garcia and his ever-vigilant police. Under cross-examination by Captain Garcia the prisoner had confessed to being a spy and a saboteur in the pay of the subversive and traitorous faction led by the criminal Don Diego Vargas.

Landon pursed his lips. There was no doubt that they were after Diego's blood as well. He read on:

During the night the Santa Ana Gaol was broken open with the aid of high explosives. One prisoner was callously killed and two others seriously injured, simply because they got in the way of the designs of evil men. The authorities were quickly alerted, but the gaol-breakers, having a good start, were able to make their get-away under cover of darkness. It is thought that the Englishman, Harvey Landon, may try to cross the border into Argentina. Border posts have been alerted.

There was a photograph of Landon, probably taken from his passport, but it was so blurred that he felt sure no one would recognize him by comparing his features with those of the print. He pushed the paper away, finished his coffee, and walked out of the hotel.

The sun was beginning to warm the air, and there was every indication of a sweltering day ahead; it would be hot work walking the twenty or thirty kilometres to Almagro. It was still early, and few people were moving in the main street of Cabildo. Here and there a sleepy-looking man would stare at Landon with mild curiosity, but no one spoke to him, and he gave no greeting for his part. He would be glad to be clear of the town; he felt conspicuous, his feet scuffling through the rapidly drying mud, and all those silent houses with their silent eyes watching him. The street seemed endless.

A dog came at him, barking furiously, but when he showed no fear it halted and then slunk away. A peon went by on horseback, a rolled blanket slung across the front of the sheepskin saddle, a lariat hanging at the side. He did not look at Landon but stared ahead, his thin leathery face under the wide-brimmed hat showing no expreşsion. The inhabitants of Cabildo appeared to be a morose and sullen lot, probably largely of Indian blood, with all the sombre characteristics of their race.

Landon began to sweat, not so much from the heat as from the feeling of being watched. If the people he had met had been less incurious, or had spoken a single word to him, he would have felt happier. But this silence, this attitude of strict withdrawal, played on his nerves. He felt that, though in the street he was ignored, from every shadowed window he was being watched by secret people who whispered to one another: 'That is the Englishman, Harvey Landon, who escaped from Santa Ana gaol.'

Involuntarily he increased his pace, hurrying to get clear of the town.

"Hola! You there!"

The shout was like a blow in the back to Landon. He stopped walking and turned slowly round.

"Come here."

A man was standing in the doorway of a timber building that Landon had just passed. He was wearing the uniform of the Central Republican police and he had a revolver slung in a holster at his waist.

Landon's first impulse was to run. It was a natural instinct, but it was so ridiculous that he rejected it instantly. He could not hope to get away by running. Beyond Cabildo was only the road across the pampas. There was no shelter, no place in which to hide, scarcely even a tree.

He walked slowly back towards the police-station — if such the building was. He had hoped that a place as small as Cabildo might not have boasted such an establishment, and perhaps it did not. Perhaps the policeman was simply visiting Cabildo; perhaps he had been born there. It made no difference.

He was a young man, black-haired and not very tall. He looked athletic, and the hands resting lightly on the cartridge belt around his waist were capable, strong-looking hands. He had soft black eyes and a moustache like a pencil stroke across his upper lip.

"You wished to speak to me?" Landon said in a cold, dispassionate voice.

The policeman had been resting his right shoulder against the doorpost. He shifted across the doorway and leaned on the other shoulder.

He asked: "Where are you going?"

Landon hesitated a moment, then said: "To Almagro."

The policeman looked at Landon's feet, at the short riding-boots with the trousers pulled down over them. The boots were muddied and they were not ideal for walking; they were made for use in stirrups.

"It is a long way — to walk."

"I like walking."

The policeman nodded. He did not make any remark on this peculiarity of taste. He seemed to accept it without question. "It will be hot — very hot. You are Americano?"

Landon almost replied: 'No — English,' when he had second thoughts. He said: "Yes — Americano."

"Where have you come from?"

Landon thought swiftly, remembered a signpost at the other end of the street, and replied with only the smallest hesitation: "From San Luis."

"Why do you walk? Have you no car?"

It was a difficult question to answer. Surely all Americans were rich, had cars, and would not willingly walk half a kilometre. An American on foot was an anomaly, an object of suspicion — appearing so suddenly in a place like Cabildo at this hour in the morning, even more suspicious.

Landon said: "I have friends with the car. I walk to Amalgro for a bet. You understand?"

The policeman grinned suddenly. A bet; yes, he could understand that. Besides, it was well known that all Yanquis were mad.

"By God! I would not walk it even for a bet." He looked at Landon's soiled clothes, and again the breath of suspicion rose in the hot, still morning air. "You have had an accident perhaps, señor?"

"I fell down. It is nothing."

Landon drew a packet of cigarettes from his pocket, some that Don Diego had given him. "You will have one, Captain?"

The policeman was flattered by the swift promotion. He accepted one of the

61

cigarettes. "A thousand thanks, señor."

Landon took one also, and the policeman lit the two of them.

"And now," Landon said, "I must be on my way."

He had gone no more than ten yards when the policeman stopped him again with a shout. Landon turned, and the policeman came towards him, the cigarette in his mouth and the revolver swinging from his hip. He walked with a swagger, as though with pride in his authority and power. Landon waited.

"I have just remembered," the policeman said. "An American car went through half an hour ago. It was perhaps your friends."

"Perhaps," Landon said.

He turned and walked away from the policeman. He wanted to look back, but he willed himself not to do so. He could imagine the policeman standing there in the middle of the street, gazing at his receding back. The man had sounded friendly, but there had been something in his soft black eyes that spoke of doubt, of suspicion. Admittedly all Yanquis were mad. Nevertheless . . .

# 4

## The Road to Almagro

THE sun rose higher in the cloudless sky, drying the puddles in the road. A haze of steam ascended into the air. Landon took off his jacket and slung it over his shoulder; then he loosened his tie and unbuttoned the collar of his shirt. The shirt clung sweatily to his back.

It was less a road than a track, strewn with boulders, pockmarked with potholes, tufts of grass growing between the wheel-marks. It did not appear to be a busy road. Landon encountered one or two mounted peons, and a group of Indians who went padding past, their bare feet raising little spurts of dust from the dried-out surface, their gaze bent upon the ground, on their backs heavy bundles which they carried without apparent distress in the scorching heat. Two vehicles drove by in the direction of

Cabildo, a cloud of dust following them like some phantom that had dared the light of day. A vulture floated in the sky on wide, strong wings.

Landon reckoned that he must have been walking for nearly two hours when he saw the car. It was parked at the side of the road; at least, he supposed it to be parked until he came closer and saw that both back wheels had sunk into the ground as far as the axle. There was a tree beside the road at this point; one of the few trees that Landon had seen on his journey; it had probably been planted there for shade. He felt that he could do with a little shade, for the sweat was coursing down his face and neck.

There were three people standing by the car — a man and two women. They were all young — in the early twenties, Landon judged. They were staring at the back of the car, and they did not notice Landon until he was close enough to speak to them.

"Having a bit of trouble?" He spoke in English because he had seen the plate on the back of the car proclaiming its country of origin as the United States, and he guessed that these must be the Americans that the policeman in Cabildo had told him about. He had had no thought then of catching them up, but now that he had by chance managed to do so his mind was already busy with ideas of how he could make use of this piece of fortune.

The three looked up and saw him. The man was tall and red-headed, with a well-nourished look in his freckled face. One of the girls was a red-head too, with the flawless complexion that often goes with such hair; it was easy to see that she was the man's sister. The other was small and dark, vividly beautiful; both of them were dressed in thin cotton frocks, and were bareheaded. The man was in blue jeans and a check shirt open at the neck.

He said: "Well, how d'you like that! A fellow American?"

"English," Landon said.

"You live hereabouts?" the American asked. He gave a sweep of his arm, indicating the rolling grassland with no sign of a house or even a hovel. "Don't tell me that." He grinned in a friendly way.

"I'm on a walking tour," Landon said dryly. He pointed at the car. "How did you get into this mess?"

"We stopped for a meal. When we came back to the car there she was, stuck."

It looked to Landon as if the rain of the previous night must have undermined the road at the spot where the Americans had had the ill fortune to stop. The weight of the big car had caused the ground gradually to subside beneath the rear wheels until further subsidence had been halted by the axle.

"Got a spade?" he asked.

"There's one somewhere in the outfit."

"We'd better start digging then."

"We?"

"I'll lend you a hand if you'll give me a lift into Almagro. Is it a bargain?"

The American looked him up and down, probably noting the sweaty, unshaven appearance, the dried mud on boots and clothing. Landon was aware that he looked a tough customer. But after one glance the red-headed American opened the car boot and unstrapped a spade.

"I'd have taken you anyway," he said, "but I'll be glad of some help with the digging in this heat."

It took them an hour of steady toil to free the car, by the end of which time they were both drenched in sweat. The girls dispensed bottles of 'Coca-cola,' and Landon drank thirstily, gladly; it seemed a long time since he had had coffee in the Hotel Alameda.

While they laboured the Americans gave information about themselves. They were on a tour of South America, a round trip beginning and ending in Buenos Aires. They had started by pushing westward across Argentina, over the Andes into Chile; then they had travelled north along the coast to Bolivia, had turned east, and now were on the last stage of the journey.

"You found good roads?" Landon asked.

"Roads! It'd be flattery to call them that. Compared to some of those tracks this is Broadway."

As Landon had already guessed, the red-haired girl was the man's sister; the other was his wife.

"My name's Swindon," he said. "James Elroy Swindon; but everybody calls me Red. What's your name?"

Landon hesitated, caution curbing his tongue. The fewer people who knew who he really was the safer it would be. Even these Americans might talk, might see his name in the papers, might give him away.

"My name's Harvey," he said.

The American repeated the name. "Harvey. Sure, but we've got to call you something, and we don't go much on formality. You've got another name."

"Call me Joe," Landon said.

Mrs Swindon's name was Jacqueline — "Jackie to my friends!" The red-headed girl was called Gloria. She had a deep, pleasant voice and a slow, drawling manner of speaking; she looked capable and self-reliant.

"Gloria is our navigator," Red told Landon. "And boy, have we needed one!"

Gloria was also the interpreter, the only one of the three who spoke more than a word or two of Spanish. Landon, resting from digging, looked at her with interest.

Despite the sweltering heat, she looked cool; he wondered how she managed it. He was acutely aware of his own unwashed, unshaven, sweaty condition. Looking at this tall, attractive girl, he wondered momentarily, and not for the first time, whether there was in the final assessment much to be said for the kind of existence that he led: six years of war at sea, a wound in the stomach from a German shell splinter, the D.S.O.; and the rest of his life spent in wandering, poking his nose into other people's troubles, skating on thin ice, moving on the borderland of illegality, sometimes in the money, more often out of it.

It had all seemed fine enough once, fine and romantic and exciting; but lately he had begun to have doubts. He was no longer young. Where was his future? What had he got for all his pains? A wound in the belly that could still on occasions double him up with agony, a piece of ribbon, the promise of five thousand dollars as soon as he contacted Mr Delgado, and a host of memories that a smarter man might have made into a best-selling book. Well, it was all right; all right for most of the time. But just now and then you saw a girl like this Gloria Swindon and you began to wonder: might there not have been a better way?

She saw him looking at her and noticed the corrugation in his forehead. She said: "You look worried, Joe. What's the trouble? Running away from the police?"

He felt annoyed that she should have to call him Joe, which was not his name, and annoyed with himself for having been caught staring at her.

"No trouble," he said. "Nothing to worry about." He took the spade from Red's hand and began to shovel earth from under the car.

They arrived in Almagro just before mid-day.

"We're staying here for the night," Red told him, "then crossing the border into Argentina to-morrow. Where do you want to be dropped?"

"Anywhere," Landon said. "It doesn't matter."

He left them in the centre of the town

and was sorry to see them go. With them he had felt safe, as though the powerful hand of the United States was stretched protectively over him. Now, alone again, he had to rely on his own resources. Well, he had always done so, and they had always proved sufficient; he had never needed anyone to fight his battles for him. All the same, he was sorry to say good-bye to the red-headed girl.

Almagro was a town of some size, big enough to afford cover for a hunted man; it was not the kind of place where a stranger is immediately noticed. Landon decided to do as the Americans were doing and stay there for the night, crossing the border in the morning. Unfortunately, it would not be as simple a matter for him as it was for them, armed as they no doubt were with passports and visas and every other necessary document and paper.

Landon had not made any definite plan, but he had a hazy project in his head of hiring, or if necessary buying, a horse or mule, riding out to open country where the border was not likely to be patrolled, and slipping across. He did not know whether this was feasible, but for the moment he could think of no better way.

The first thing was to buy some kit. At present he had only the clothes he stood up in, and he could hardly go to a hotel with nothing in his hand. Even in a border town like Almagro the hotel staff might look at him askance. Therefore he set out at once on a shopping expedition.

Two hours later he was washing the sweat and grime from his body under a shower-bath in the Hotel del Sud and feeling a hundred times better. He stepped out from the shower and began to dry himself, grinning sardonically as he caught sight of his reflection in a full-length mirror fixed to the wall of the bathroom. He saw a lean, muscular body, the shoulders rather too wide for perfect proportion, and the arms a little too long. He saw a narrow waist and flat stomach, with the great white ruck of the scar stretching from the naval to the left hip where the shell splinter had ripped him open. He saw slightly bowed legs, thin legs like those of as cavalryman, and each also with its legacy of scars. Not a pretty body, he thought — not a likely winner in a male beauty contest. Yet it went well with his face; they were both tough and lean and bony. Perhaps his character was like that too — tough and lean and bony, if such words could describe a character.

At least his face looked better for having been shaved: the outline was no longer blurred with stubble, the hard angle of the jaw was smooth. He had bought toilet gear, pyjamas, a shirt, underclothes, shoes, and a zip-fastened canvas bag. With these possessions he felt more confidence in himself; he was not so much a vagabond now.

He finished dressing, went back to his room, dragged a comb through his stiff hair, still damp from the shower, and walked slowly down the hotel staircase. The clerk was busy at the reception desk; he looked up as Landon went past, gave a nod, and bent again over his accounts.

Landon went out into the afternoon sunshine. He could have done with some more sleep, but he could not bring himself to sleep in the hotel room during the day. Shut in by the four walls of the room, he had experienced a sudden feeling of claustrophobia. It was like being in prison again; he could so easily be caught there, trapped without hope of escape. He preferred the open air.

Almagro was a town of contrasts. In the modern part were wide, well-paved streets, with trees planted along the pavements and four- or five-storey buildings of concrete and glass. The old town was like a poor relation hanging on to the skirts of the rich, a sprawling eyesore of corrugated iron shanties and adobe hovels, dirty, ragged children playing in the dust, and gloomy Indians spreading their merchandise at the feet of passers-by. Yet it was in this less hygienic but more picturesque quarter that Landon found Gloria Swindon.

He saw her before she noticed him. She was haggling with a sad-faced Indian over the price of a little figure carved from some brown, fine-grained wood.

"Hello there," Landon said. "I didn't expect to see you again."

She turned, with the carving in her hand, and stared at him, wrinkling her

74

forehead, as though she did not recognize him. Then she smiled — a warm, friendly smile.

"Why, Joe; it's you. At first I didn't know you. You look — different."

"I've shaved," he said dryly.

She flushed, for a moment losing something of her poise. "I'm sorry. I shouldn't have said that."

"No need to be sorry. What have you done with the rest of the party?"

"I lost them. They're around somewhere. I'll join them later at our hotel."

Landon said: "How about wandering around with me?" He felt that he needed a companion to distract his thoughts, to keep his mind off the idea of pursuit. Every time he saw a policeman the thought came into his head that perhaps this man would recognize him, that he would feel a hand laid heavily on his shoulder as he moved through the crowd. But, quite apart from this, he would have been glad of the company of Gloria Swindon at any time. Nevertheless, having made the suggestion, he almost regretted it. Suppose she did not wish to accompany him, made some excuse?

He would feel a damned fool. And why should she want to walk round Almagro with a man like him, a man she had met only that morning tramping the road like a hobo?

She did not hesitate a moment, however. "Why, that would be just fine. I'll pay for this funny little man and then — "

"Let me buy it for you." Landon said.

She protested, but he overcame her objections. He still had plenty of Don Diego's money left, and he was able to beat the Indian down to a far lower price than she could ever have reached. He had practice.

"I can never do that," Gloria said. "I guess I'm just weak-willed or something."

"You don't strike me that way," Landon said. He was carrying the carved figure in his hand as they moved away from the vendor. "I'd say you had a very powerful will — guessing, you know."

She looked at him, still smiling. She was almost as tall as he was, and he could see the high-lights in her burnished hair;

it seemed to have borrowed some of the radiance of the sun. He wondered how she kept it so well under control; the living must have been rough at times on the tour. If it came to that, how did she manage to preserve that wonderful complexion?

"Perhaps I have," she said. "I usually get what I want."

"And know what you want also?"

"Usually."

Already, as they wandered through the streets of old Almagro, making their way gradually back to the glass and chromium of the new town, Landon felt the relaxed calmness of this girl having its effect upon him. The tension inside him eased; he felt less jumpy, less inclined to look over his shoulder. It was strange, this effect she had on him; he could remember no other woman who had acted on him in that way. It was almost as though he needed her, as though she made him complete. And he had never needed a woman in that particular way before. He had taken women for pleasure, for the enjoyment of the moment, and had let them go again without regret. They had never been part of his life. But this girl . . .

He pulled himself up short, putting a brake on this thoughts. He was a fool to let ideas get into his head. He was maybe twenty years older than she, a man with no prospects except the hope of five thousand dollars if he ever managed to reach New York. Hell! what did it matter? What the devil did it matter? After to-day he would probably never see her again.

He took her to one of the new air-conditioned, glass-and-chromium palaces and bought her a piled-up mountain of ice-cream and fruit.

"I have childish tastes," she said. "I love these things."

For himself he bought something less garish. An idea had come into his head, an idea for getting across the border. He wondered whether he could trust this girl, and decided immediately that he could.

He said: "My name isn't Joe Harvey; it's Harvey Landon."

He saw the little pucker of bewilderment in her forehead. "Then why did you say it was Joe?"

"Harvey Landon means nothing to you, then?"

The pucker was still there. "No. Should it?"

"If you'd read the local papers you might have noticed it. Harvey Landon is wanted by the police. He broke out of a gaol in Santa Ana."

She put down her spoon and stared at him across the table. "You're not kidding, are you?"

"Do I look like a kidder?"

"No," she said; "I don't think you do. What were you in gaol for?"

"Revolutionary activities."

"Oh, that." He could see the relief in her expression. "I thought it might have been something criminal."

"In this country it is criminal — at least, in the eyes of the government. Now I have to get across the border, and I haven't a passport."

The pucker had gone from her forehead, but she was not smiling. She dabbed at her ice-cream with her spoon, as though it no longer attracted her.

"Are you asking me to help?"

"That was more or less the idea."

"How?"

"Your brother has a big car. You're going into Argentina to-morrow. The border officials aren't likely to worry you. America puts too much money into this country."

"You want us to take you? But you'd be seen. They won't let four go through for the price of three, and if you haven't got a passport — "

"Cleopatra was carried to Caesar rolled in a carpet."

"Cleopatra?" She looked puzzled for a moment; then she laughed. "Oh; I see. Do you think it could be done?"

"It could be done all right if you and the others agreed."

She was silent for a while, thinking, turning the matter over in her mind. Landon feared that she was going to reject the proposal; it was, he had to admit, a lot to ask of some one you had only known for half a day. But after calmly considering the question she answered evenly: "Very well. We'll do it."

"Can you speak for the others?"

"Yes," she said; "I can."

She was, Landon had to acknowledge, no ordinary girl.

★ ★ ★

He had hardly stepped inside the lobby of the Hotel del Sud when he knew that something was wrong. There were two men in the uniform of the Central Republican police leaning on the reception desk and talking to the clerk.

Landon entered quietly, and none of the men noticed him. The backs of the policemen were turned towards him, but there was a big mirror behind the reception desk, and in it he could see the reflection of their faces. One of them had a dark, heavy face, blackened with sprouting beard around the chin and cheeks. He had pushed his cap back from his forehead, and it was possible to see the white line of the scar encircling it, disappearing behind the ears.

He was talking in a soft, rapid voice, and the clerk was listening.

It was Captain Garcia.

# 5

## Across the Border

LANDON was suffocating inside the carpet, the sweat pouring from his body. He felt sure that it could only be a matter of time before the sweat began to trickle out from the ends of the roll and betray the presence of something else besides the carpet in the back of Swindon's car. He hoped the border officials would not take too long in passing the Americans through.

Landon had to abandon his newly bought possessions in the room at the Hotel del Sud. He had taken one look at Garcia's reflection in the mirror behind the reception desk, and then he was out of the door in double quick time. A street-car happened to be passing; he avoided death from a motor lorry by inches, leaped on to the street-car, and rode on it for the length of ten blocks. Then he got off, ran down a side-street, turned two more corners, and saw the entrance to a cinema. Without hesitation he bought a ticket and went in.

Sitting in the cinema, he felt reasonably safe for the moment. He was fairly sure that Garcia had not seen him; there had been no sign of pursuit as he boarded the street-car; no one had dashed after him from the hotel. There could, nevertheless, be no question of going back to claim his things. True, he had checked in under a false name, but the clerk had looked at him in some surprise, noting his dirty and unshaven appearance, which might have barred him from a more exclusive hotel. The clerk would have remembered him and would no doubt have told Garcia, who would not be slow to put two and two together. Possibly they would search his room; they would find his discarded shirt and boots, and Garcia might recognize them. No, it would not be safe to go back.

Landon stayed in the cinema until it closed, sleeping for the greater part of the time. It was nearly midnight when he came out into the streets, and somehow he had to get through the night. He went to a rather dinghy eating-house and bought himself a meal, lingering over it until he felt that to stay any longer would be to make himself conspicuous.

The streets were now becoming deserted, and if he did not wish to make the police take notice of him it was imperative that he should go to earth. Then, in a yard between two buildings, he saw just the thing he was looking for — a parked motor lorry with a canvas hood over the back. The yard was open, and there was nobody about. Landon put his hands on the tail-board, gave a jump, got one leg over the top, hauled himself over, and dropped to the floor of the lorry.

He landed on something yielding, yet bony — a man's body. The body swore at him and rolled away. Landon lay down on the floor of the lorry and heard men snoring in the darkness. He was not the only one among the poor and destitute of Almagro who had chosen this spot for a night's lodging.

He slept poorly. His bedfellows produced between them a stench that was almost overpowering; fleas transferred their attentions to his body, biting unmercifully. He shifted his position and found another man's face pressed close against his own, the hot, evil-smelling breath flowing over him. He rolled over and found his knee pressing into another man's stomach; the man mumbled in his sleep and put an arm over Landon's shoulder, drawing him closer. Landon pushed the fellow away, groped towards the tail-board, and squatted in the corner with his knees drawn up to his chin.

He was glad when morning came, and one by one his companions of the night began to drift away, taking their rags, their vermin, and their stench into the light and sunshine of another day. He went to an early-opening eating-house and revived himself with coffee and crisp rolls hot from the baker's. He smoked a cigarette and bought a morning paper from a barefooted urchin who came running into the café, crying his wares. He had time to spare, and he read the paper through from front to back, but there was nothing in it concerning himself. He left the paper in the eating-house and went to find a barber's shop, where he could get himself shaved.

He met the Swindons as he had arranged with Gloria, and he could see at once that Red was not pleased with the arrangement. There was no welcoming smile on his freckled face.

"Gloria tells me you want us to smuggle you over the border," he said. "Now that's a pretty tough assignment. It's breaking the law. There could be trouble."

Landon said: "You don't have to do it if it scares you. If you want to call it off say so. I'll find some other way. I don't want to persuade you into anything that seems too dangerous."

Swindon coloured. "Who said anything about being scared? It's just that — "

"Of course he'll do it," Gloria cut in in her cool voice. "I promised you he would. He's just feeling sore because you didn't ask him first."

"I don't want him to do it if he'd rather not," Landon said. "I don't want to get anyone else into trouble. I've made enough for myself."

"Oh, heck!" Swindon burst out. "Let's not stand around arguing the point. Let's go and buy that goddam carpet."

Landon knew when the car reached the Central Republican customs post beyond Almagro. The car stopped, and he heard Swindon and the girls get out and bang the door. That was the prearranged signal for him to keep still and make no sound. It was not too easy; he was slightly doubled up, and his back had begun to ache. He wanted to stretch out his limbs and, above all, to take a breath of good fresh air; he seemed to be breathing carpet, sucking it down into his lungs. He thought of Cleopatra and wondered what kind of state she had been in when she arrived before Caesar. If her experience had been anything like this she must have been pretty ruffled, but, from all accounts, she had impressed Caesar none the less for that.

It was fortunate that the car was wide; the other three had been able to travel in the front quite comfortably, leaving the whole of the back free for him and his carpet. American cars had their advantages. But he could feel the sweat on his back, on his legs, trickling through his hair; he could taste the saltiness of it on his lips. He hoped he would not have to endure it much longer.

He heard the door of the car open and a man's voice, not Swindon's, saying something; but he could not catch the words. Then the door banged again and there was silence, and after what seemed like a day and a night to Landon in his hot and sticky confinement the others came back, got in, and the car started up.

"That was O.K.," Swindon said. "They were as sweet as honey. Never suspected a thing. Hoped we'd had a good time and would come again. Somehow, made me feel mean."

These remarks were addressed to Landon, but he made no reply from his muffled retreat. Swindon could feel mean if he liked; if he had been in Landon's position his outlook might have been considerably altered. Landon was not surprised that the customs officials had been easy. An American passport was treated with respect; it might be sycophantic respect, but the result was the same. The United States poured a good deal of money into the Central Republic, and General Romero's government had issued orders that its officials were to treat all Americans as privileged persons. It was knowledge of this fact that had first given Landon the idea of passing across the border in Swindon's car.

"Now for the other lot," Swindon said.

The Argentine customs post was only a short distance from the Central Republican one, and after a few minutes the car stopped again. Landon was apprehensive that things might not go so smoothly with the Argentines; they might be on the look-out for contraband, might even search the car. But his fears were groundless; the officials stamped all the documents without delay and did not even trouble to look inside the car. Within half an hour they were across the border, driving on an Argentine road, and Landon was able to come out from his carpet and gulp with greedy lungs the clean air flowing through the windows.

"You look ruffled, Harvey," Gloria said.

"I feel as if I'd been in a Turkish

bath. I'm certainly glad to be out of that carpet. I never want to be rolled up in another one as long as I live."

"It was your idea," Swindon said. He seemed to have become more cheerful now that the border had been crossed. Landon guessed that he had been more worried than he would admit. It was only Gloria's influence that had persuaded him to go through with it. Landon was grateful to her and wished that he could express his gratitude, but he had not the gift of graceful thanking.

He said awkwardly: "You've all helped me a lot. Now you can drop me as soon as you like."

"Where's the hurry?" Gloria asked. "I though you said you were going to Buenos Aires."

"So I did."

"We're going there too. You may as well come with us. You won't get there faster any other way."

Landon saw Red glance at his sister. Perhaps he would have liked to be rid of the intruder at once. Perhaps he did not trust Landon. He could be excused for not doing so. After all, Landon was a self-confessed gaol-breaker, a revolutionary; he might, for all Swindon knew, have other crimes to his name.

But Red made no open objection. "Sure," he said, "we'll take you into B.A." If his tone was not exactly welcoming it was not hostile. He seemed to be taking a neutral position, as opposed to his sister's pro-Landon one, reserving judgement. Jacqueline did not enter the discussion; she seemed to leave every decision to the two red-headed Swindons, agreeing without argument to everything that they decided on between them. Pretty and vivacious, Landon concluded, but easy-going, no match for the strong wills of the others.

"What do you aim to do in B.A.?" Swindon asked. "If it isn't an indiscreet question."

Landon hesitated a moment, saw Gloria's cool, interested gaze fixed on him, and came to the rapid conclusion that there was no point in making a secret of his proposed movements.

"I'm travelling on to New York. I have business there."

Jacqueline cried delightedly: "Why, that's where we're going. We live there."

"You do?"

"Sure, sure," Swindon said. "We're flying. Leaving the car to follow by sea."

"I hope to fly too. The sooner I'm in New York the better. I want to get the business done with."

"Important?"

"Important to me — financially."

"How will you manage to leave this country without a passport? It may not be too simple. You can't fly to New York in a carpet."

"I'll find a way."

Perhaps he would — and again, perhaps he would not. Much depended on Señor Alvear, Don Diego's agent in Buenos Aires. It was Alvear who was to provide Landon with money for the flight to New York. He had a letter for Alvear in his pocket as well as the one for Delgado. Perhaps the agent could arrange something about a passport. "José Alvear is a clever man," Diego had said. "If you ever want any tricky business doing José is the one to do it."

"Is he safe?" Landon had asked.

"Safe? Harvey, my friend, you can trust José like your own brother. He is devoted to our cause. And, what is more — an even stronger argument perhaps — it pays him very well. Oh, no, you need have no fear of José."

★ ★ ★

Three days after crossing the border the car was gliding through the busy streets of Buenos Aires. On either side the buildings of the great South American city towered above them, and Landon felt that he had reached the end of the first stage of his journey. The five thousand dollars were coming closer.

He did not go to the same hotel as the Americans; it looked far too expensive. Until he could tap Señor Alvear for some pesos he had only the money that he had brought out of the Central Republic; he had, therefore, to find for himself something a good deal more modest than the Plaza.

This was far from being the first time he had been in Buenos Aires, and he knew of a place where accommodation was cheap and where they would not ask questions about such things as passports and identity papers. That was where he would go.

His first concern after leaving the Swindons was to change the remainder of his Central Republican money. He found an exchange bank and came out with 1220 pesos. It was enough to last him for a few days if he lived frugally, but not nearly enough for a sea passage to New York, let alone an airway ticket. He bought some clothing and a fibre suitcase to replace the kit he had lost in Almagro, then boarded a tram which took him, swaying and clanging, down towards the South Basin. He left the tram, walked briskly for about ten minutes, and found himself outside the establishment he was seeking.

It was a lodging-house of rather dingy appearance, much frequented by seamen and other vagrant characters. On the pavement four children — two white, one black, one coffee-coloured — played some intricate game with chalked squares and balls of silver paper, completely oblivious of passers-by, cut off in their own strange world of make-believe. In a door-way on the opposite side of the street a Chinaman sat, shaded from the sun, smoking a big-bowled pipe. A girl walked past, clicking on high heels, her black cotton dress stretched tightly across firm breasts, her glossy black hair reaching to the shoulders. She kept her gaze on the pavement, glancing neither to right nor to left, as though intent on her own thoughts. The Chinaman took his pipe out of his mouth and spat into the gutter. Two flies — fat, blue, metallic-looking — settled on the tight-curled wool of the black boy's head; he was either unaware of their presence or did not care, for he made no movement to drive them away. A cat came out of the lodging-house entrance, and Landon walked in.

He found an old, crease-lipped, black-sheathed woman in a hot, dark little cupboard of an office, who looked up at him with beady eyes, questioning.

"I want a room," he said. "Two nights — three — maybe longer." He drew fifty pesos out of his pocket and put them in her vein-ridged hand. She looked at the money, then back at him.

"Mariner?" she asked.

"Yes."

"Number fifteen. Second floor."

She handed him a key with a metal tab attached to it. He picked up his suitcase and went up the creaking, carpetless stairs, a smell of stale food cooking, dirty clothes, and bad drainage filling his nostrils.

Number fifteen was a room so small that a fat man would have found difficulty in squeezing between the iron bed and the plain, white-painted dressing-table. A window in the wall opposite the door was tightly closed and fastened, so that the room had become a box of hot, stale air. Landon dumped his suitcase on the floor and pushed the window open. Below was a yard strewn with broken crates and garbage bins, the bins overflowing and swarming with flies. A stray dog, nosing hungrily in the overflow, gave a frightened leap in the air as it heard the window grind open; then it returned to its scavenging. An iron fire-escape zigzagged down the wall of the lodging-house; it had an appearance of rust and great age.

Landon turned back to the room. He sat down on the bed and listened. A sound, rising and falling with a steady, regular beat like very distant waves rolling in on a shingle beach, came to his ears. For a while it puzzled him; then he realized that it was some one snoring in the next room. Somewhere some one was plucking at a guitar — idly, as though the player too were half asleep. Everything seemed drowsy with the heat — even the flies, crawling like black filth upon the surface of the window, even the spiders that had hung their webs in the corners like safety-nets ready to catch any plaster that might fall from the cracked and yellow ceiling.

Landon changed his shirt and smoked a cigarette. He heard the mournful hooting of a ship's siren coming up from the river in reverberating waves of sound. The afternoon was slipping away, and it was too late to hunt for Señor Alvear; that job would have to wait until to-morrow.

Landon felt as drowsy as the flies and the spiders. He kicked off his shoes, lay back on the bed, and went to sleep.

When he awoke it was evening, and his mouth was dry. He put on his shoes and jacket and decided to go out in search of a drink.

He was about to descend the stairs when he heard the sounds of what appeared to be a fierce argument between the old woman and a man who had just come in from the street. The first sight Landon had of the man was the top of his head and his shoulders. It was a large head, covered with an untidy thatch of black hair, and as the man talked his head swayed backward and forward, flinging the hair over his eyes.

"What in blazes are you wanting now, you old heathen?" he shouted. "What is it, hey? Why can't you speak a Christian language, damn you?"

The old woman replied with a torrent of rapid Spanish, waving and gesticulating with her thin, claw-like hands, as though at any moment she might entirely lose her self-control and throw herself on the Englishman, tearing at his throat with her nails.

"To hell with you, then; to hell with

you!" he yelled. "I'm damned if I can make head or tail of what it is you want."

He was turning away from her in exasperation when Landon reached the foot of the stairs. He was a very tall man and very thin, with stooping shoulders and concave chest, as though the weight of his massive head and its load of black hair had gradually become too much for the body to support. The face was thin and long-jawed, the nose curved like the beak of a parrot, and the eyebrows joining in one thick, unbroken line across the bridge, like a slice off the tail of a black cat.

"What's the trouble?" Landon asked.

The man seized Landon's arm, shaking it vigorously. "English, by God! Damn me if I'm not glad to hear a civilized tongue. Now, tell me, can you understand what this old hag is saying, for I'll be hung if I can get a slant on her meaning?"

The woman had fallen silent for the moment. Now she began again, aiming her words at Landon. He listened to her for a few minutes, then silenced her with a word and turned to the tall man.

"She says you owe money for your room. You paid for a week and you've been here two. Is that right?"

"Oh, yes, it's right enough. Well, if that's all — " He thrust a hand into his hip pocket and pulled out a wad of dirty paper money, from which he peeled some half a dozen notes and gave them to the old woman. "Here, take it and be damned to you."

She grabbed the notes, counted them, handed one back, and disappeared into her cupboard.

"Old witch," said the tall man without malice. "You'd think I was trying to cheat her." He looked keenly at Landon. "You staying in this dump?"

"Yes," Landon said.

The man nodded. He had a very wide mouth and a long, flexible upper lip; the nose curved in towards it as though to pin it in place. His ears were large and set almost at right angles to his head, like studding-sails put out to catch the lightest breath of wind. His eyes were quick-moving and intelligent.

"Name's Green — Jonas Green. If you

want anything just ask. I'll be glad to help."

"Right," Landon said. "I will."

He watched Mr Jonas Green climbing the stairs to his room. Then he went out in search of a drink.

# 6

## A Question of Money

SENOR JOSÉ ALVEAR leaned back in his chair, a long, thin cigar projecting from his sallow, fleshy face, his hair smoothed down with oil and shining like polished ebony. His fingers, much beringed, were interlaced across his stomach; his eyes were heavy-lidded, half-closed. He seemed to be almost asleep.

"So, Señor Landon, you have a letter from my good friend, Don Diego Vargas. May I have it?"

Landon pulled the letter out of his pocket. He pushed it across the wide expanse of the heavy mahogany desk to Alvear, past the gold inkstand, the embossed leather blotting-pad, the cut-glass paper-weights, and the silver cigarette-box. Prosperity, even wealth, was obvious in all the fittings of José Alvear's office. There could be little doubt that he would be able to supply the pesos that Landon required.

And the passport? There was a certain shiftiness in Alvear's eye, a slyness hidden beneath the external sleepiness of manner, that indicated a willingness and probably an ability to carry out transactions that might not be completely legal. Who better than a lawyer to dabble in illegalities? Perhaps that was the kind of man you needed as the agent of a revolutionary movement.

Alvear picked up the envelope and slit it open with an ivory paper-knife. He took out a single sheet of rustling paper and with a murmured, "Your pardon, señor," began to read. After a while he refolded the letter, put it carefully back in the envelope, and dropped it on to the desk. Then he pressed the tips of his fingers together and gazed at Landon over the gathered ash on the end of his cigar.

"So," he said at last, "you are bearing a letter to Señor Delgado in New York."

Landon nodded, watching Alvear's eyes, their lids drooping.

"And you require money."

Landon nodded again.

Alvear sighed. "Unfortunately it is not possible. I cannot supply you with any money. No, none at all."

Landon stiffened in his chair. "But Don Diego said — "

Alvear made a fluttering motion with one hand; the gold rings glittered in a beam of sunlight from the open window on one side of the room. "What Don Diego said is, I am afraid, beside the point. Since he wrote this letter there have been changes. It is no longer possible for me to lay my hands on the sum you require."

"You can let me have nothing?"

"Nothing."

Landon thought he could detect the smell of treachery. Diego had said that he could trust Alvear like a brother, but he had also hinted that it was money that kept the agent faithful. Suppose he had found a way of making more money by being faithless? Alvear did not strike him as a man who would hesitate at the double-cross if it suited his own purpose.

He probed a little farther. "There was

also the question of a passport."

"A passport?"

"My own was taken from me in Santa Ana. Don Diego said that you might be able to provide a — substitute."

A spasm passed over Alvear's face. One might have supposed that he had been shocked. "That, of course, is even more impossible. I cannot imagine how Don Diego could have supposed I should be able to help you in that respect. There are laws; one has to observe them."

"Not every one is deeply concerned with such observances — especially when it is to their advantage not to be."

Alvear shrugged, but not so violently that it brought any creased to the fine, lightweight jacket that he was wearing. "There are perhaps such persons; I cannot say. I should not wish to have dealings with them. For myself, I take care — very good care — not to become entangled in any transaction that might lead to unpleasantness. I am sure you see my point, do you not?"

"I see that you are a double-crossing scoundrel," Landon said, without raising his voice.

Alvear's eyes glittered momentarily, but he showed no other sign that the insult had touched him. His voice when he answered was as smooth as ever.

"Let us have no hard words, please. They serve no useful purpose; they are merely inflammatory." He tapped with his fingertips on the desk, gazing at Landon, as if sizing up his man. "Perhaps we could come to some amicable agreement. It might, after all, be within my power to assist you — financially. The passport is, of course, quite another matter."

Landon was on the alert. The smell of treachery had become stronger. "Go on," he said.

Alvear leaned back in his chair, but he did not take his half-closed eyes from their task of observing Landon's face. "You have a packet, a letter, to deliver to Delgado in New York, but it appears to me that you are going to find that task somewhat difficult — yes, very difficult, in fact. Now, I could perhaps relieve you of the burden. I think I might find a way of delivering the letter for you. How does that proposal strike you?"

Landon said coolly: "I was to receive five thousand dollars from Mr Delgado on delivery. Are you prepared to pay me as much for treachery?"

Alvear raised his hands in horror. "Who spoke of treachery? I assure you that in my hands the letter would be far safer than in yours. I assure you also that it would be delivered to the appropriate quarter."

"What do you mean by that?"

"Just what I say — to the appropriate quarter. Now, Señor Landon, let us understand each other. You are an adventurer — shall we say a soldier of fortune? Does it matter to you from what direction that fortune comes? Of course it does not; it is the money that counts. Am I not right?"

"I think you are speaking for yourself."

"For you also, I believe."

"And would another paymaster be prepared to pay five thousand dollars?"

Alvear tipped ash from the cigar into a silver ash-tray flanked by a silver model of a mounted gaucho. "Five thousand dollars is a great deal of money; as things stand at present you cannot have any certainty of obtaining such a sum. It is as matter of much speculation."

"Don Diego assured me — "

"Don Diego assured you that you would obtain money and a passport from me, did he not? Yet you have obtained neither. Do you not think that the assurances of a man who has had to flee to the mountains for refuge are slender foundations on which to base one's future? I make myself clear perhaps?"

"Very clear."

"Well then, seeing that the five thousand dollars you expect to receive for your pains in New York — when you reach that city — are of such an uncertain quality, would it not be in your own best interests to take, let us say, one-fifth of that sum here and now, and consider the task completed?"

"No," Landon said.

Alvear's eyebrows rose slightly. "No? I beg you not to be over-hasty in coming to a decision."

"There is no question of coming to a decision," Landon answered coldly. "You have called me an adventurer and a soldier of fortune. Both descriptions may be correct; I am not ashamed of them. But there is one thing that no one has yet been able to call me, and that is a traitor. So you see, Señor Alvear, even if you were to offer me five thousand dollars, or ten thousand, the answer would still be the same. I gave my word to Don Diego that I would deliver the letter to Mr Delgado in person and allow it to fall into the hands of no one else. As long as I am alive and able to do so that is what I intend to do."

"As long as you are alive." Alvear's voice was smooth, musing; it was almost as though he were speaking to himself, allowing his thoughts to form themselves into words without any conscious will. "That might perhaps not be so very long."

Landon said harshly: "Are you threatening?"

"Señor Landon, it is not for me to threaten. I am a peaceable man. I think I may truly say that I have never willingly inflicted physical suffering on any fellow creature. The very idea of pain sickens me; the sight of blood is enough to make me thoroughly ill. Unfortunately I cannot speak for others. There are certain men who would stop at nothing — nothing whatever — to gain their ends. It is of such men that I would advise you to beware."

Landon kept his anger under control. The only sign that there was any in him was the drumming of his blunt, strong fingers on the arms of his chair. Alvear did not recognize the sign, or did not heed it. It was Alvear's belief that all men were to be bought, this one no less than any other.

"Let us say two thousand dollars — payable in cash. Two thousand dollars and a whole skin are surely preferable to a very problematical five thousand and the distinct possibility of some — ah — mishap."

Landon despised this man, this sleek, sleepy-looking, cat-like man who had been content to take money from Don Diego and his fellow revolutionaries when it suited his purpose, and then had not hesitated to slide over to the other side when it appeared expedient to do so. Or had he perhaps been a traitor always, taking his pay from both sides and betraying one to the other?

Landon said coldly: "I've lived long enough and dangerously enough to know how to take care of myself. I've given you my answer."

He got up, pushed the chair away, and walked to the door. Alvear made no attempt to detain him. He merely said: "I think you are a fool."

"The opinion of dog's vomit," Landon said, "does not interest me."

He shut the door behind him and went down the stairs and out of the building into the hot sunshine of early January. He breathed in deeply, as though to flush out of his lungs the oppressive, treachery-laden air of Alvear's office. At least he knew now where he stood; he knew that he could not look to Alvear for help, that he would have to depend upon his own resources.

He had much to occupy his mind as he wandered aimlessly through the busy streets of Buenos Aires, with cars and buses speeding past, intent, so it seemed, on running down any pedestrian who might be foolhardy enough to venture away from the safety of the pavement. No one took any notice of him; he was alone with his problem — the problem of how to get from Buenos Aires to New York without a passport and with no more than a few pesos with which to pay his fare.

He thought of the British Consulate, but dismissed the idea at once. Consular officials were inclined to look with disfavour at men like Landon. He knew what would happen if he went to the Consulate; if not turned away from the door, he would be met with the bleak civility of officialdom, with questions that it might be difficult to answer satisfactorily. They would want to know just what he had been doing in the Central Republic, how he had come to lose his passport, how he had got into Argentina without it. The Consulate was for law-abiding citizens, not for such as he.

He pondered Alvear's scarcely veiled threats. He was not fool enough to suppose that they were idle. The letter that he possessed was important; it was important to the revolutionaries that it should reach Mr Delgado, and it was equally important to the Central Republican government that it should not do so — that it should instead fall into their hands and yield its secrets to them.

Landon saw now that it would have been prudent not to have gone to Señor Alvear at all. Until that visit he had been reasonably safe in Buenos Aires, because no agent of the Central Republic was aware that he had crossed the border. Now they would not only know that he was in Buenos Aires, they would know also that he carried a valuable letter. He had enough experience of such people to be sure that, as Alvear had said, they would stop at nothing to prevent that letter reaching its destination. And one certain way of preventing such an event was surely by killing the courier.

Landon came to a crossroads and saw an Argentine policeman directing the traffic from an island with the help of a whistle and much gesticulation. The police! They were no use to him; he could not go to them for help, for he had already put himself outside the law.

He was an illegal entrant; he had broken out of a gaol in Santa Ana; he might even be wanted for the murder of the prisoner who had died. If he went to the police they might very well arrest him and send him back to the Central Republic. There was nothing for it but to fight his own battle, and for the moment he could see no way out.

But meanwhile the sun was shining, and he had arranged to have lunch with Gloria Swindon. He pushed his problems to the back of his mind and made his way in the direction of the Plaza de Mayo.

Gloria had bought a new dress. She looked, thought Landon, like somebody who had just stepped out of an advertisement for some beauty aid. No one would have imagined that she had travelled thousands of miles over the rough roads of the pampas and the rock-strewn highways of the Andes.

"I don't know how you manage it," he said.

"Manage what, Harvey?"

"Whatever the situation, you look cool, unruffled, and very lovely."

She looked at him with an expression

114

of pleasant surprise, as though she had been given an unexpected treat.

"Why, Harvey, you said that very nicely. I didn't know you could make such a graceful little speech."

"I meant it," he said.

"That makes it all the nicer."

Lunching with her, listening to her voice with its not unpleasing American accent, seeing the laughter in her eyes and the sheer zest for living in her every movement, every expression, Landon tried hard to forget his own problems. But they would not leave him. He wondered how quickly Alvear would act, how quickly he would pass on the information that he had gained. Perhaps already the net was closing, even as he sat here frittering away his time. Time might be invaluable. It was no longer safe in Buenos Aires; the sooner he was out of the city the better. But how to get out?

"We're leaving to-morrow," Gloria said.

Landon's head jerked up. "So soon?" He had hoped that they would be staying longer. This day might be the last time he would see her — if things went wrong.

"The air line had cancellations, so we were able to get tickets. Red is arranging transportation of the car right now."

"I was hoping you would have had a few days here."

"I was too; but Red is keen to get back home now. He's got work to do. We've been away a long time."

"I'll have to say good-bye to-day, then," Landon said.

"Not good-bye, Harvey. You'll come and see us when you get to New York. Promise that."

"Nothing would hold me back," he said. Yet he knew there was something that might, something beyond his control.

They spent the rest of the day sight-seeing like any couple of tourists, gazing at statues and monuments and public buildings. They examined the Obelisk that had once caused so much dissension in the town council and had shed most of its outer covering the day after school-children in a massed choir had sung songs around it. "Like the walls of Jericho," Landon said, "it just came tumbling down." They looked at

Government House, the famous Casa Rosada, at the Pirámide de Mayo commemorating the Argentine Republic's independence from Spain, and the statue of General Belgrano. They moved on to the Law Courts and the Colón Opera House, to the Botanical Gardens, and, finally, the Zoo.

"Doing the rounds," Gloria said, smiling. "Isn't that supposed to be typical of American tourists?"

"In Europe they have something of a reputation," Landon said. "Half an hour for the Tower of London, twenty minutes for St Pauls Cathedral. As a nation you're supposed to be great hustlers."

"Life's so short. There's never time enough for everything you would like to do."

"True. Here to-day and gone to-morrow — that sort of thing." He thought of to-morrow, when Gloria would be gone, and there was a bleakness in the prospect that made his heart sink. Hell! he thought. Don't tell me I'm falling for this girl! He would be a fool if he thought there could be any future in that. He had no illusions about himself; he was no longer young, and, like Henry the Fifth, he had never looked in a mirror for love of anything he saw there. Could he imagine that a girl like Gloria Swindon would be attracted by that hard, bony face, with its thin, sardonic mouth and weather-beaten skin? She had accompanied him this afternoon because there was no one else. Back in New York things would be different.

"When do you expect to leave Buenos Aires?" she asked.

"When?" He gave a brief, humourless laugh. "The Lord only knows. When — and how? Those are the questions."

She looked into his face, her eyes serious, a little worried. "Harvey, you're not in trouble, are you? I mean — that business in Santa Ana, it's all left behind now, isn't it?"

He grinned reassuringly. "Of course — all left behind and forgotten."

There was no reason to saddle her with his worries. To-morrow she would be flying north in all the luxury of a great air-liner, while he would still be here in Buenos Aires, like a caged animal hunting for a way out. But there was no reason why she should know the threat that was hanging over him. He alone had brought it on himself; alone he would face it.

He said: "It may take a few days to fix things up, but there's nothing to worry about. I shall probably travel by ship, so don't expect me for a while."

"I shall be looking for you," she said. "I'll show you New York."

"That will be fine," he said.

It was late when he left her. Before he went she said: "You may kiss me if you like." Then, as he hesitated, she added: "You've been wanting to, haven't you? Don't tell me I've imagined it, Harvey."

He had wanted to, but he had held back, knowing that if he kissed her, if he once held her in his arms, he would be lost; he would never be able to get her out of his mind. She would be there, plaguing him. And he did not want her in his mind; he wanted it free to deal with other problems — problems of life and death. This other matter was something else, something that he had no time to attend to.

It was dark where they were standing,

but he could see the pale outline of her face, the thick mass of her hair, looking now almost black.

"Gloria!"

He ought to have pushed her away; he knew he was making a damned fool of himself. But there was no help for it. He put his arms about her and drew her to him. She came unresisting. Now he knew she would be on his mind — always.

★ ★ ★

The stairs of the lodging-house creaked under his weight as he climbed to his room. There was only one low-powered light burning, and there were shadows on the stairs. He had to grope his way down the passage, hunting for number fifteen, and striking matches to read the numbers on the doors.

He found it at last, pushed the key in the lock, and let himself in. He shut the door behind him, switched on the light, and saw at once that he had had a visitor.

His fibre suitcase was lying open on the bed, its few contents thrown aside. The covers had been ripped off the bed, the mattress turned up, and the drawers of the dressing-table all pulled out. Whoever it was who had made the search had done it thoroughly and in haste, but he had not found what he was looking for.

He? Landon sniffed the air. There was a faint yet perceptible odour of cheap perfume hanging about the room. Had his visitor then been a woman? He thought of the old hag below, but dismissed the thought. She had her own smell, but it was not like this.

He put a hand to his jacket and was reassured by the feel of the crisp envelope in the inner pocket. He looked at the disorder in the room and was glad that he had not left the letter there. And yet the door had been locked. How had the intruder got in? He looked at the open window and guessed the answer; the fire-escape provided an easy back way. He had been a fool to tell Alvear where he was lodging, but he had not then realized that Alvear was a traitor. The fellow had lost no time. The hunt was on.

# 7

## The Shadow

LANDON was having his hair cut when he first noticed the little man in the dark-blue suit. The man was sitting behind him, waiting for his turn with a number of other customers, and Landon could see him in the barber's mirror. The man had a thin, abnormally narrow face, with a drooping lower lip, like a piece of rubber that had lost its elasticity and would no longer keep in place. His hair was lank, brown, and greying at the temples; the suit looked too big for him, as though it had been made for some other person, or as though he had shrunk since having it made. His whole appearance, in fact, seemed shrunken; it gave an impression of insignificance and self-effacement.

He was staring at the back of Landon's head with a curiously steady, unwinking stare, as if intent on engraving the exact contours permanently on his memory. It was his eyes that shocked Landon. Something stirred in him, raising the goose-flesh; he experienced a feeling of revulsion. He had seen eyes like that somewhere before; as the barber's scissors snipped away he tried to remember where.

After a while he had it. It had been in a little town in Normandy. The police had arrested a man in the street — had plucked him up from under the nose of the passers-by and handcuffed him in a moment. He had been an insignificant-looking man in drab clothes, rather ragged; yet he had, so Landon was to learn, murdered no fewer than eighteen people. He was a maniac, a pathological killer. For a moment Landon had stared into his eyes. They had a dead, stony, sightless quality; they might have been the eyes of a corpse. The eyes of the man in the blue suit were like that.

The man did not realize that Landon had seen him; he was not looking at the mirror. After a moment he took a tobacco pouch out of his pocket and began to roll a cigarette with meticulous care. His hands were small and white and delicate, like the hands of a woman. Landon, head bent forward to allow the barber to perform, watched him in the mirror, still with that queer, cold feeling of revulsion quivering in his spine. It was the kind of revulsion some people had for toads, others for snakes or spiders. He felt as if he needed to wash his hands, to wash away the very presence of the man.

The barber finished Landon's hair. Landon got up and went out of the shop, not looking at the man in the blue suit. When he had gone some way down the street he glanced over his shoulder and saw the man also leaving the shop. Perhaps he had become tired of waiting; that was the least unpleasant explanation of his appearance.

He looked first to the left, then to the right, as if undecided which way to go; then he began walking in the direction that Landon had taken. He walked with a peculiar kind of dragging shuffle, scarcely lifting his feet from the pavement, and his left shoulder seemed to be lower than his right.

Landon went down a side-turning and walked with a sudden increase of pace. When he glanced back, however, he also saw that the man in the blue suit had also turned the corner and was, despite his dragging shuffle, moving fast also. Landon stopped and looked in a shop window; the man stopped too and began studying the traffic with an absorbed air. When Landon moved on he followed.

There could be no doubt now in Landon's mind that he was being shadowed, and very clumsily shadowed at that. Either the man was a tyro at the job or he was so contemptuous that he was not even attempting to veil his actions. Somehow, for all his threadbare, badly fitting suit, his thin, unremarkable features, and his shuffling gait, Landon did not think he was a tyro. He remembered the eyes, and he decided there were other men he would rather have had on his tail.

He came to a souvenir shop in which he had once bought a wallet, and on a sudden impulse he went inside. There were no other customers in the tiny shop, and the proprietor, who traded under the name of 'Harry' and advertised himself in handbills distributed among all the British ships in the port as 'Purveyor of Hy-class Curios, Butterflie-wing Orniments, Alygater Handbegs and Solid Silver Ashtrees. English Spook,' came forward with a beaming smile of welcome.

He was a hand-rubbing, bowing-and-scraping little sparrow of a man, with a trim moustache and mobile, jet-black eyes. Either he had an excellent memory for faces or he was a very good businessman, for he greeted Landon as if the Englishman had but a moment since stepped out of the shop; whereas, in fact, five years had passed since Landon was last there.

"Ah, my good friend. So you come back. Fine, fine."

"You remember me?" Landon asked.

"Remember you, kind sir! Who could ever forget a face so distinguish? A gentleman out of the top bloody drawer, as we say. No?"

"No," Landon said.

"Oh, well; what matter? Top, middle, bottom. You are welcome, sir, welcome to my 'umble emporium." He spread his arms in an all-embracing gesture. "What to-day is it, sir? A bag for the young lady's 'and, a lamp-shade made from genuine armadillo, a tray of superb butterfly wings made with my own two 'ands in my own workshop? What is it to be, sir? Take your choice, but do not 'urry. Among so many treasures, 'ow to choose — what a problem!"

Harry's hands fluttered above the treasures like two of those blue and yellow and purple butterflies whose gaudy wings had provided the decoration for so many of his trays and trinkets. He was eagerness, boyishness, salesmanship, all rolled into one. It would have stabbed Landon to the heart to have gone away without buying even so much as a filigree brooch; to have told the man that his merchandise was all worthless, shoddy trash would have been to inflict a bitter wound upon his self-esteem.

"You are 'ere for long, good sir, in Buenos Aires? Your ship, it is in port some fine big time, off the filthy, rolling sea?"

"What makes you think I'm a sailor?" Landon asked.

Harry clasped his hands together, the fingers twining. "Ah, good sir, as if I do not know a sailor — me what is once steward on board a Blue Star liner. No, good sir, there is no fooling little 'Arry. I know a sailor when I see one."

Landon peered over his shoulder and saw that the man in the blue suit was standing outside the shop, staring with those bleak, dead eyes at the trinkets in the window. His face was completely expressionless — an unhealthy, pallid face, apparently untouched by the sun. He must have seen Landon glance at him, must have realized that Landon knew he was there and that he was following. He had made no real attempt to mask his purpose. It would have been ridiculous if it had not been so menacing.

Landon picked up a cigarette-lighter. "How much is this?"

"That, sir? Ah, there you 'ave one damn fine lighter. One, she is lit; two, she is out. In all of Buenos Aires, if you search for twenty year, you will not find

128

a better. Sir, I tell you something about that lighter; you may not believe, but it is true — "

"Tell me the price," Landon said.

"The price!" Harry appeared saddened that anyone should wish so soon to descend to such mundane and sordid questions before the whole poetic beauty of the article had been described. The price already! He shrugged, made a motion with his expressive hands as if he were weighing invisible money-bags, and said: "The price, good sir, is thirty pesos — thirty pesos only for an article worth five times as much. It is only because of my great love and regard for all sailors — all English sailors, that is, and you, sir, above all — that I bring myself to ask so ridiculous a price. I shall be the loser; but what of that? The great joy of serving such a gentleman as yourself, good sir, will reward me ten thousand times over."

"I'll take the lighter," Landon said.

When he left the shop the man in the blue suit was still looking into the window, motionless, apparently completely oblivious of all that went on around him. When he had gone a short distance Landon glanced back. The man was shuffling along behind him.

Landon became suddenly very angry. It was not simply the fact of being shadowed that roused his anger; it was that the thing should be done so openly, with so little regard for secrecy. It was as though the fellow were mocking him, playing a game of cat-and-mouse, amusing himself at Landon's expense. Not that he appeared to derive much amusement from his occupation. It would have been difficult to imagine laughter coming from so sombre a creature; a smile would have been an incongruity worthy of remark.

Landon had had enough of the passive rôle that had been allotted to him. It was not in his nature to allow others to dictate the course of events. He turned suddenly and retraced his steps. He had reached the man in the blue suit before the fellow had time to move away. When he found himself face to face with Landon he would have stepped to one side, but Landon put out a hand and gripped his arm, preventing him. He seemed to shiver slightly at the touch of Landon's fingers; his arm was thin, scarcely thicker than a broomstick under the threadbare cloth of the sleeve, and Landon's grip was merciless.

"Why are you following me? What's the game?"

There was no expression on the man's face, neither anger nor resentment — least of all, fear — just nothing. His cold, dead eyes stared at Landon — seemed to stare through him, as though he had not been there. Landon was close enough now to see that there were pockmarks in the pallid skin and a strange slackness at the corners of the mouth. The man's collar was dirty and limp. His tie, of a nondescript brown colour, was creased with much use, the small, tight knot slipping away to one side.

And then Landon noticed something else about the man; he carried with him an odour of cheap scent, the odour that had been apparent in the room at the lodging-house. It was sickly, nauseating. Landon's nose twitched with disgust. But he knew now he had made no mistake in tackling this man.

He shook the arm. It was like shaking the limb of a scarecrow, and it had as much effect.

"Out with it, then. Who are you working for? Who set you on to this game?"

The man made no reply, but he did not attempt to release his arm from Landon's grip. He was completely passive, content to wait. Again Landon felt that peculiar revulsion that he had experienced earlier. He let his hand drop. This man was surely subnormal, lacking in the ordinary human reactions. Yet it was that very subnormality that made him all the more dangerous. Such a man would kill without any of the feelings of pity or remorse that a normal man might feel. It was such men as this who became the paid murderers, the hired thugs, gaining perhaps some gruesome satisfaction from the act of killing, as though they were thus striking back at that society from which their subnormal bodies and their warped minds made them outcasts.

"Damn you!" Landon said. "Can't you answer? Have you lost your tongue?"

The man in the blue suit swallowed,

and his Adam's apple went up and down in his scraggy throat like a yo-yo on a string. But he said nothing.

Landon became convinced of the futility of trying to get any information from this man. What could he do? Beat him on the head with clenched fists? Grip his neck and shake him until some normal feelings were shaken into his brain? It would all have been useless. As it was, his interrogation was beginning to attract attention. He turned away in disgust and began walking rapidly in the direction of the Paseo Colón. When he looked back he saw that the man in the blue suit was still following.

He decided to shake him off. He jumped on to a passing bus, travelled ten blocks, got off, plunged down a side-street, rounded three corners in quick succession, boarded another *colectivo*, rode past twenty blocks, got off, and went into a cinema.

If the man in the blue suit had been able to follow him through all those moves he was a far better exponent of the art of shadowing than he appeared to be.

Landon settled down in his seat and prepared to watch an American film with Spanish sub-titles. He had come in half-way through and he had no idea even of the name of the film, but that did not worry him. He had entered the cinema not for entertainment but because he was sick of being followed. In the cinema he could rest his legs, cool down in the conditioned air, and think over his problems slowly and calmly.

"Perdóneme, señor."

Landon looked up and saw a man trying to get past. The man was small and round-shouldered; he shuffled past Landon and sat down two seats farther on.

"Gracias, señor."

Landon sat down again, feeling cold. That man — could it have been his shadow? He dismissed the thought. It was not possible. If he was going to imagine every half-seen, round-shouldered figure to be that man with the drooping lip he was going to have a bad time of it; he would be for ever looking over his shoulder. He had to take a grip on himself.

The essential thing was to think of some way of getting to New York. Not until then, not until he had contacted Mr Delgado, would the five thousand dollars be his; and not until then could he see Gloria Swindon again. How to get to New York? Flying was out of the question, and land travel was impossible. There remained only the sea — without money, without a passport. Stow away on board a liner? It might be possible. In the absence of any more likely plan it would bear looking into.

He stayed in the cinema a long time, resting, thinking, scarcely looking at the screen, occasionally going out in to the foyer to smoke a cigarette. When he left it was late in the evening, and beginning to grow dark. He bought himself a meal in a cheap eating-house and began to walk back to his lodgings.

After a while it became evident to him that he had missed the way. He found himself in an area of dark, gloomy buildings that might have been warehouses. There were railway lines underfoot, let into the road, and he guessed that he must have wandered down to some part of the town bordering the docks. He halted, trying to get his bearings. There was a strange feeling of desolation about those tall, shadowy buildings, these deserted railway lines, during the day no doubt so busy, but now abandoned for the night.

Completely abandoned, it seemed, for there was no one in sight. Here and there, at wide intervals, street-lamps cast pools of light; between were shadows, gloomy doorways in which a man might lurk unseen. The idea that he was being secretly watched came into Landon's head. He tried to cast it out immediately. He was letting his imagination play tricks again; he had to watch it, keep it under control. But the idea persisted.

He could not remember ever having been in this part before, and he was not sure which direction to take in order to get back to his lodgings. Then he heard some one approaching from behind, and he turned towards the sound of the footsteps with the intention of asking this person, whoever it might be, to direct him on his way. But he did not ask, for suddenly he realized that these were dragging, shuffling footsteps, and that the man whose grotesque, wavering shadow was thrown forward by the street-lamp at his back was the man in the blue suit — the shadow.

Landon stood absolutely still, looking at him, and the man came on, not hurrying, but moving purposefully forward, as though he knew exactly what he had to do and was ready to do it. He had one hand in the pocket of his jacket — the right hand. When he was no more than ten yards from Landon he drew that hand out of the pocket, and there was something in it, an object which in the uncertain light was difficult to see clearly.

But Landon knew what it was. He flung himself to one side just as a spurt of flame shot out from the man's hand like a glowing red finger stabbing the darkness. Then Landon was running fast, bent low, zigzagging along the railway lines. He heard the pistol fire again. It seemed no more than a small cracking sound, not loud at all; but he heard the bullet go whining away into the night. He dodged round the end of a truck just as another bullet clanged on the iron of one of its wheels. He ran along the wall of a warehouse, found a doorway, pushed on a massive door, and felt it give under his weight. He slipped through the gap and went into the echoing darkness inside. Then he pressed himself back against the wall by the door and waited, breathing hard.

He heard the dragging footsteps, speeded by an attempt at running, and the sobbing breath of his pursuer. He heard the man come to a halt and knew that he was puzzled and wary. He waited, controlling his own breathing, keeping silent. Two cars raced past outside, seeming to belong to a different world, and he heard a rat scamper across the floor of the warehouse. He thanked his stars that the door had been left unfastened. Then he saw the shape of a man outlined dimly in the opening.

Landon jumped him and chopped him down with a hammer-blow of the fist before he could use his gun. He went down like a sack of meal, suddenly limp. Landon kicked the gun into the darkness and left him there. He went out of the warehouse and saw a taxi coasting down the road. He stopped it and got in quickly.

"Take me to the bright lights," he said. "Take me anywhere if it's got lights and music and drinks."

The taxi-driver grinned. "English sailor?"

"Yes."

"I know the place to take you — just the place." He let in the clutch, and the taxi shot away at speed. Landon leaned back in his seat, sucking his knuckles and thinking of a rat in a warehouse — a rat in a blue suit.

# 8

## Jonas Names a Ship

LANDON had a double whisky. He felt that he needed it. He drank it quickly and ordered another. With the new drink in his hand he found time to look around him, to get into focus this night-spot to which the taxi-driver had brought him. If he had been carried in blindfolded he felt he could have made a pretty accurate guess at the set-up simply by the taste of the whisky; the barman called it Scotch, but Landon would have laid a sizeable bet that it had never been within five thousand miles of Scotland. The night-club — so called — was in keeping with the liquor; it was raw and shoddy.

The room in which Landon found himself was long and rather narrow. At one end the bar was presided over by two thin, slick-haired barmen in dirty white jackets who looked about as happy as mourners at a funeral, and at the other end a five-piece dance band, protected from contact with the customers by a kind of chromium-plated cattle-fence, maintained an almost unbroken blare of music. Along each of the longer walls were little partitioned alcoves with tables and padded seats, and on the cramped central piece of floor space a number of couples were dancing with the sad, absorbed expressions of participants in some pagan ritual.

In one corner near the band some half-dozen women in evening dresses that looked well enough at a distance but might not have borne too close an inspection waited with the bright, expectant look of females who know that their livelihood depends upon their ability to attract the male.

Landon began to wonder why he had come. It would have been better to tell the taxi-driver to take him straight back to his lodgings. Here the whisky was bad, the noise deafening, and the atmosphere was so hot and smoky that is seemed to press upon the lungs like a dead weight.

He had been in places like this before; they varied little from port to port, and for him they had lost the attraction of novelty. In them you frittered away the money you had earned at sea; in return you got amusement, a kind of enjoyment perhaps, a thick head, and maybe something worse. He decided to finish his drink and go.

Then he saw the tall, thin man from the lodging-house — Jonas Green. Green was half drunk; his eyes were bloodshot, his hollow cheeks unnaturally flushed, his black hair falling untidily over his forehead. But he had wits enough about him to recognize Landon.

"Well, if it ain't my good friend who speaks Spanish lingo. Tasting the bloody night life of B.A. Is that it?"

He winked heavily and nodded once or twice very wisely, his beaked nose seeming to peck at the air in front of him.

"I'm just going," Landon said.

"Just going! Man, you can't do that. I'm going to buy you a drink: that's what I'm going to do. A drink. Now, what's it to be?"

"I don't want a drink. I've had enough."

"To hell with that for a tale! Why, I can see with one look at you — one look — that you're as sober as a flaming judge. Am I right?"

"You are."

"Well then, what's all this talk about leaving? Damned nonsense. You've got to drink with me. I insist that you drink with me, Mr — hell now, if I haven't been and forgotten your bloody name."

"You haven't forgotten it. I didn't tell you. But it's Harvey Landon." There was no point in concealing the fact now. He was a marked man, in any case.

Jonas Green drooped over Landon like an overburdened sapling. He put a hand on Landon's shoulder and spoke with all the ready, irresistible matiness of the man who is at least half-way in liquor.

"And a bloody fine name too. I defy anybody to say it ain't — anybody." He glanced around, as though trying to find somebody who was prepared to argue the point, but was disappointed. "Harvey Landon, eh! Well now, Harvey, what's it to be? Between two true-blooded

Englishmen in a damned crowd of foreign bastards. We hang together, you and me, like brothers — twin brothers. Is it whisky, then?"

"I told you I didn't want any more," Landon said. He was getting a little tired of having Jonas Green leaning on him, but short of pushing the man off by force he could see no way out of the predicament.

"If it's the money you're thinking about," Green said, "forget it." He felt in his pocket and hauled out a thick wad of notes. "Plenty of pesos — loads of the muck — and only the one night left to spend it in. To-morrow I go aboard. Just between our two selves, Harvey boy, I've got a ship. So now you name that drink."

"Very well," Landon said. "If that's how it is I'll have another whisky." The mention of a ship had made him think twice about getting rid of Jonas Green. This would bear looking into. There might be a chance for him also.

Green slapped Landon's shoulder. "That's the boy. We'll make a night of it, you and me." He signalled to

144

one of the sad-faced barmen. "Two whiskies, sonny." He held up two fingers so that there should be no mistake. "Dos — whiskee — pronto."

"This ship," Landon said. "What is it?"

"A tanker."

"Sailing north?"

"For sure. She's light now. She'll go north to Venezuela and pick up a cargo of petroleum for Philly — at least, so I been given to understand."

The whiskies came, and Green paid for them. "Look," he said; "why strain our legs when we can sit down? Let's take a seat. Maybe we have some female company. What you say?"

He drew Landon into one of the alcoves and looked towards the group in the corner. Two of the girls detached themselves from the bunch and made their way to the alcove. Landon decided that they had looked better at a distance. Perhaps he had not drunk enough of the rot-gut whisky. Green seemed to find them attractive enough. He leered at them.

"Sit down, girls. Make yourselves at

home." He patted the seat beside him in a gesture of invitation. One of the girls sat down next to him; the other attached herself to Landon.

A waiter appeared as if by magic. The girls ordered wine, and Green paid.

"They get a rake off," Landon said. "They'll be drinking champagne before you've finished. It's all part of the lovely business."

"Why, sure they do; but what the hell! Everybody's got to live, and I've got money to burn. It's the last night. Make it a good one, I say."

He turned to the girl beside him, a plump, fair-haired girl in a pale-blue dress, cut low at the neck to reveal her best points. "You speak the English, no?"

The girl shook her head, smiling at him with her lips, her eyes dull, tired-looking. She had thickly pencilled eyebrows, and the hair was swept back from her forehead and tied with a ribbon at the back of her neck. When she smoked one of Green's cigarettes her lipstick stained the paper so that it looked as though she had been bleeding at the mouth.

146

"You know one sort of language all right, I'll be bound," Green said. "All your sort know that." He put a long arm round her waist and squeezed her.

"About that tanker," Landon said. "Are there any more vacancies in the crew?"

Jonas Green's face came away from the region of the fair-haired girl's ear. He stared at Landon, surprised. "Are you on the beach too? I never thought of that."

"Yes, I'm on the beach."

"Well, well, well; why didn't you say so?" The girl snuggled up to him, but he pushed her away. "Now, hold it, kid, hold it. Plenty of time for that later." He spoke to Landon again. "Sure, I think there's room for more. The way I heard it, five of the crew scarpered — set off to make their fortunes on a bloody treasure hunt or something inland. They'll be lucky. Now the ship's near ready to sail, and they're wanting crew bad."

"Do you think they'd take me on? I've got no papers."

Green gave Landon a look of surprising keenness. He was, Landon concluded, not half as drunk as he gave the impression of being.

"So it's like that, is it, Harvey boy? You've been in trouble." He gave a laugh. "Well, what's that? So have I. I've got no clean discharge. But men like you and me is what this sort of ship is looking for. The *Gloria del Mar* ain't particular concerning things like good characters. She takes what comes, and not too many questions asked neither."

"*Gloria del Mar* — is that what you said?"

"That's it. You heard of the tub?"

"No — no. I've never heard of her." The name — Gloria; it was a coincidence, perhaps a good omen. Gloria, the girl, had helped him to get across the border into Argentina; perhaps Gloria, the ship, would help him to get away from Buenos Aires.

"What nationality is she?"

"The flag," Green said, "is Panamanian. The owner's a Greek — a millionaire, so they tell me."

"A flag of convenience," Landon said. Well, that was the right kind of ship for him. No trouble about a discharge book

148

or papers of identification. Sign on, and no questions asked. Low wages, maybe, but no prying.

"And the officers?"

"The captain's English, but I don't think he would get command of an English ship. Name of Sharpe. You ever heard of 'Brandy' Sharpe?"

"No."

"He was in bad trouble once — years ago. Ran his ship on a reef and broke her back. Turned out at the inquiry that there was no proper watch being kept. Sharpe was in his cabin — drunk on brandy. That's how he got his nickname. But that was years and years ago; I haven't heard nothing about him since. Maybe he's sobered up. He ain't so young now. Though I never heard tell of age sobering a man what was gone on his drink."

"How do I get in touch?" Landon asked.

"You're serious about this? You really want to sign on? It may be a tough berth; I'm warning you."

"Do you think I'd be afraid of tough berths?"

Green looked at him, and again there was that keenness in the glance, giving the lie to drunkenness.

"No; I'd say not. But why the flaming hurry to get clear of B.A.? If that's not a rude question."

"You may as well know," Landon said. "A few more days here and I don't think I'd be wanting either a tough berth or a soft one. Six feet of earth would be enough. This evening a man shot at me. He shot to kill."

Green whistled softly between his teeth. "So that's how it is. Boy, you certainly need to get away. You come with me to-morrow. I'll guarantee you get taken on."

The plump girl wriggled closer to him and the band went into a new dance tune. Green stood up and pushed the girl out on to the dance floor.

"I want exercise," he said. "Come on, kid."

Landon watched them move away. Green could dance. On the floor he seemed suddenly to acquire a grace that had not been his before. His movements flowed in unison with his partner's. Landon knew that he could never dance like that. He gulped some more of the pseudo-Scotch, thinking of the *Gloria del Mar* and hoping they had not yet managed to complete the crew.

He had almost forgotten the girl at his side until he heard her say in a halting, childish voice: "You dance, pleece?"

She was small and rather thin, as though she did not get enough to eat. Landon, really looking at her for the first time, thought that she was young too, perhaps not yet twenty. She had large, wide eyes and a tiny mouth. The make-up, applied too thickly and inexpertly, had the effect of seeming an evil mask fastened upon the face of innocence. Yet Landon knew that he would be a fool to suppose her innocent. Only a fool would be misled by a face.

He said harshly: "You don't need to try your English on me. I can speak Spanish."

She looked startled, as if he had purposely kept this ability to converse with her in her own language a secret, and now had sprung it on her like a trap. "I am sorry, señor. I didn't know."

151

"Of course you didn't. How could you? Dance, you say. Well, why not? If I'm bad at it why should you worry? Why should any of us worry about anything? Can you tell me that? No, you can't; you can't tell me anything. That's not what you're here for, is it? It's not your job."

He could feel the effect of the bad whisky rising to his head; and perhaps there was, too, a reaction after being shot at. Some of those damned bullets had gone close. He looked at his right knuckle; the skin was broken, and it had bled a little. He held it out for the girl to see.

"Look; a man's jaw did that. He would have killed me if he could. Do you know what it feels like to be near death? It isn't pleasant."

Too many times he had been close to death, had felt the cold grave-breath upon his neck. A twinge of pain gripped his belly, reminding him. Yes, there had been that time too. He seized the girl's hand and held it, waiting for the pain to go. She stared at his face, and he could see that she was scared. Perhaps she thought him mad; perhaps he was mad. What was madness? What was sanity? Was the man in the blue suit mad or sane?

The pain passed like a cloud passing away from the face of the sun. His grip on the girl's hand relaxed. He smiled, trying to reassure her — this child.

"Come along, then. Let's dance."

He moved stiffly. He could feel her slender child's body under the thin material of her dress. Her breasts were small and firm, pressing against his chest. She had a kind of animal odour, an odour of body-sweat and warm breath and cheap scent. Her cheek against his own was smooth and soft, like Gloria's. The music beat upon his eardrums in brassy waves of sound, like an ocean pouring over him, engulfing him, carrying him away in its great flood.

He had no consciousness of moving his feet; it was as though the floor shifted under them, the walls, the ceiling moving round of their own volition like the interior of a shadow-show, circling, weaving. The other dancers passed across his line of vision like creatures in a dream, out of focus, coming close, then receding. And the music went on and on, so loud and blaring that it was almost tangible; he could almost feel it, as he could feel the girl's body pressing hotly against his own.

Then the pain came again, and he knew it was going to be one of those bad spells that he sometimes had; he did not know why. Perhaps the surgeon had left some pieces of splinter in his belly, some bits of iron that dragged their claw into his flesh. He did not know why it was, why the pain came; but he knew when it was coming. At such times he liked to be alone; he did not care for anyone to see him fighting this battle with pain.

He said: "I've had enough of this. I want a drink."

Perhaps whisky would deaden the pain. But he knew that it would not. It never had.

He went back to the alcove and moved up into the farthest corner close to the wall. The girl followed him, obediently, like a dog at his heels. He drank the whisky he had left and said to the girl: "Get me some more — quick!" And he pushed some money into her hand, not troubling to count it.

She brought the whisky, and he drank again. The stuff burned his throat, but it could not burn away the claws in his belly, the groping iron claws that seemed to be tearing at the walls of his flesh. He gripped the table, digging his fingernails into the wood, and the sweat stood out on his forehead.

The girl asked anxiously: "Are you ill, señor?"

Perhaps, Landon thought sardonically, she wondered whether he was going to die — there, in front of her in that alcove with its padded seats made for lovers to sit on, whispering in each other's ears. It would be something to die there, with the brazen trumpeting of the dance band for a funeral dirge, with the hired girls and the sad-faced barmen and all the fools spending their hard-earned money on wretched liquor and so-called pleasure to stare and point and giggle in embarrassment.

But he was not going to die, not yet. He was only going to be racked with agony, torn in the guts with pain so bad that he would wish to scream blue murder till the very ceiling cracked above his head. But he would not do that either; he would not scream, would not even groan if he could help it.

"No," he said, grinning, like a dog snarling, baring his teeth with a lift of the lip. "No, I'm not ill. Don't be afraid. Take no notice."

The pain caught at him. The table creaked under the grip of his hands. The sweat began to pour down his face in streams.

"Think nothing of it — nothing."

The girl said: "Is there anything I can do? Can I get you anything?" There was concern in her childish voice, and her wide eyes gazed at him with concern also.

Through the mist of his pain Landon saw the expression on her face. Perhaps she does care, he thought; perhaps she really has some feelings. He had not considered her as a human being, some one with a background, some one who had played the games of childhood, had hopes, dreams, ambitions — maybe still had. He had seen her only in the setting of the night-club; she was something

156

fixed in that setting, not to be separated from it, not to have a daylight life at all.

He realized suddenly that Green and the other girl had come back. Green said: "Hell! you look bad. What's wrong, old pal?"

Landon could feel the sweat dribbling down over his mouth and chin; he could taste the saltiness of it on his tongue. But the pain was going; it was easing gradually, as though the iron probes were being softly withdrawn from his body. He knew how it would be; the agony would go, leaving only a dull ache like indigestion and a feeling of weariness, as though the effort of fighting the pain had drained his energy as thoroughly as a ten-mile race. That was how it always was.

He eased his grip on the table — slowly, not giving the pain a loophole, an opportunity to spring suddenly back and catch him off his guard.

"I'm better now," he said. "It's trouble I get now and then — in the guts."

"It must be bad to make you sweat like that."

"Yes — it is — bad — rather bad. It's

an old wound. They left some iron in, I think."

He was sliding his hands away from the table, daring to breathe more freely. The pain subsided, grumbling. He took out a handkerchief and wiped his face.

"Have some more whisky," Green suggested. "You look as if you could do with a bracer."

"Yes," Landon said. "I think I could." He leaned back against the padding of the seat, savouring the joy of release from pain. For a while it would seem as though this was all that man could wish for — not to be racked with that awful, flesh-rendering agony, as though nothing else mattered but the passive enjoyment of a lack of pain.

He did not dance again. He sat there with the girl beside him, drinking whisky and letting the sounds of music and talk and laughter surge over him. He drifted into a state of half-dreaming. He saw the childish, wide-eyed, scarlet-lipped face of the girl, but he saw also the plump face of Captain Garcia with the white scar ringing his forehead and the dark chins falling over his collar; he saw Don

Diego's lean, austere features, and the freckled cheeks of Red Swindon; he saw Gloria smiling at him, and then it was José Alvear with his sleepy gaze and crafty mouth, and then the man in the blue suit with his pallid skin and his drooping lip and his dead, killer eyes.

"Damn you," Landon muttered. "Damn you, you bastard!"

But it was only the girl looking at him; and the music had stopped, and Green had disappeared.

"You come with me now?" the girl said, touching his hand with her thin fingers. "You come with me now, señor?"

"Yes," Landon said wearily. "I come with you now."

# 9

## 'Gloria Del Mar'

CAPTAIN SHARPE looked across the table at Landon with his bright, shrewd, ferret-like eyes. Nobody farther removed from the popular idea of a hard-drinking ship's captain could well have been imagined. Sharpe was like a dried-up husk, with dry, flaky skin and dry grey hair. His face was shrivelled, as if at some time or other it had been thrust too close to a furnace, until all the flesh and the fat had been burned and melted away, leaving only a parchment envelope, creased and wrinkled over the bone of the skull.

His voice was high and squeaky, like an unoiled hinge, and as he spoke a little pointed sliver of a tongue darted in and out between the dry, cracked lips, as though trying without success to bring some touch of moisture to them.

"So you want to join this ship, eh?

D'you know anything about the sea? Had any experience? Or are you just a hobo trying for a cheap lift?"

The ferret eyes stared at Landon, brilliant and unwavering; they might have been trying to bore into his brain, trying to read his thoughts, to detect any falsehood in his answer.

"I sailed from England to Brazil in a yawl — single-handed. I think I know a bit about the sea."

Captain Sharpe's face registered no surprise. Its shrivelled surface was not one to record emotion. But his eyes seemed to narrow slightly.

"Is that a fact? Some voyage!" There was perhaps the faintest hint of respect in the voice, an admission that this man standing in front of him was not just the usual seaman with a black mark against his name, ready to sign on under any flag that would give him shelter. "Yes, quite a voyage! But we don't use sails in this kind of ship. Are you an able-bodied seaman? You've got no papers. I shall have to take your word. But I'm warning you — I'm a pretty good judge of a lie."

"I was in the Navy."

"Lower deck?" The shrewd eyes were on him, probing. This man Sharpe was no fool — even if he had allowed drink to make a fool of him once.

"I started that way," Landon said.

It was true; he had started that way, even if he had finished in command of a corvette. He would not tell Sharpe that; the fact of having once had his own command — and in the Royal Navy at that — was not calculated to endear him to the officers or the crew of a Panamanian tanker owned by a Greek.

Behind Sharpe, screwed to the wooden bulkhead, was the framed plan of a sister ship, the *Gloria del Pacifico*. Both ships had been built at Birkenhead and both were about ten thousand tons gross and twelve years old. They were not the show tankers of the Greek's fleet — he was beginning to think in terms of anything up to eighty thousand tons — but he still operated plenty of older and smaller ships; they still paid.

"Humph!" Sharpe grunted. He fiddled with a silver pencil, considered for a minute longer, and then said: "All right.

You'll do. Mind you work. I won't stand slackers."

He turned to the man beside him at the desk, the chief steward — a sleek, moon-faced man, who had been doing nothing but examine his soft white hands with the air of a connoisseur appraising some valuable work of art. Sharpe addressed him in Spanish.

"Take this man's particulars."

The steward seemed to wake reluctantly from his reverie. He picked up a pen and drew a printed sheet towards him. He looked up at Landon and spoke in a smooth, oily voice.

"Your name?"

"Landon."

The steward began to write in a neat, careful hand, the scratching of the pen sounding unnaturally loud in the hot cabin, where a single electric fan merely seemed to agitate the air without bringing any cooling breath.

The entry completed, Landon signed his name and left the cabin. He began to walk along the cat-walk towards the crew's quarters, glancing down at the wheel-valves and pipes and screwed-down hatches on the deck below him. He had never been on board a tanker before, and it was all new to him, a change from the lay-out of a man-of-war or even a cargo ship. The *Gloria del Mar* was a motor vessel, with the typical tanker arrangement of engines and funnel aft, navigating bridge and officers' accommodation amidships, and raised steel cat-walks with protecting handrails along either side stretching between poop and bridge and between bridge and forecastle.

At this moment she was lying alongside an oil-discharging jetty, dwarfed by towering storage tanks, sweltering under the hot sun which seemed to drag up all the thick, strong smell of oil. On the water oil-soaked refuse floated, and rings of oil spread out in ever-widening circles of rainbow blues and greens, undulating smoothly.

A man in a ragged shirt and patched trousers oared himself slowly past in a boat so old and rotten-looking that it seemed a wonder to Landon that it remained afloat. The oarsman stopped rowing for a moment, fished something out of the water, examined it, dropped it into the boat, and began to row again. A seabird alighted on the water and floated, rocking gently up and down. The oil rings reached towards it stealthily; it took off with a sudden flutter of wings, water dripping from its webbed feet.

The upper parts of the ship were painted white, the main deck a dark green. The funnel was yellow, with narrow circles of pale blue and a lozenge enclosing the letters ZX picked out in gold. Two lifeboats, swung inboard and sheeted down, were situated aft, and two others amidships. The vessel was about five hundred feet long and twenty-eight feet broad, with a probable cruising speed of fourteen knots. She would do, Landon thought. If she carried him safely to Philadelphia he would have no fault to find with her.

He and Green had spent the early part of the morning in buying kit — oilskins, sea-boots, woollen jerseys, dungarees, knives.

"It's hot enough now," Green said, "but it'll be winter when we get north of the line. It can be cold enough to freeze your eyeballs along the North American coast. I've had some."

Landon's stock of pesos was getting low, but he had enough left for the kit. All the same, it was time to be moving on; another week or two in Buenos Aires would have made the financial situation serious indeed — quite apart from any other consideration.

He wondered where the man in the blue suit was. He hit the fellow hard; perhaps he had broken his jaw. He hoped so. Anyway, once on board the *Gloria del Mar* and clear of the river Plate, all the Central Republican agents that ever were would have their work cut out to get him. It had been a piece of luck running into Jonas Green; and Green was a decent fellow, whatever he might have done to blot his copy-book. In a tight corner he might be the boy to have beside you. He might look thin and drooping, but when he gripped your hand you changed your ideas about him; that hand was like a steel grab.

Landon and Green had slipped through the dock gates in a provision van, having persuaded the driver by a judicious mixture of bribery and argument to let them ride in the back. The dock police opened the doors of the van and gave a cursory glance inside, but they failed to see the two seamen crouched behind a barrier of tea-boxes and sugar-sacks. Five minutes later they were on board the *Gloria del Mar*.

Landon came to the end of the cat-walk and found Green waiting for him with the kit.

"Well?"

"He took me on."

"Just like I said. Not too many questions?"

"No; not too many. He's a queer little bird, isn't he? Sharpe, I mean."

"He don't belie his name, though. You saw his eyes? Sharpe as needles. He might have been master of a crack liner by now if it hadn't been for the drink."

"He still lifts his elbow, does he?"

"Well, I don't know. I haven't had a lot to do with him. But you hear tales. You can't believe everything you hear, though. What about that steward? There's a crafty-looking piece of work. I wouldn't trust him the length of my arm. Not that I'd trust any steward, if it comes to that."

"You don't like the breed?"

"Well, it stands to reason they're out to do you if they can, doesn't it? You can't blame them for that. You'd do the same if you was in their position. But you aren't, and so it pays you to watch out for your rights and see you don't get cheated."

"You've been in tankers before, I suppose."

"Oh yes. There's not many kinds of ships as I haven't had experience of. Tankers are all right in some ways. In peace-time, that is. You wouldn't want to sail in them during a war."

"I've seen a few blow up," Landon said. "They burn well — especially petrol tankers."

Green gave him a look from the corners of his eyes, as though this little scrap of information about Landon interested him.

"You was in convoys, then?"

"Corvette," Landon said briefly. He did not wish to go more deeply into all that.

"Sweet little ships," Green said. "Very sweet little ships. There's been times when I've been right glad to see a corvette on my starboard beam." He picked up a suitcase and a kitbag. "Come along then; let's go and get settled in. We're sharing a cabin. That suit you?"

"Suits me fine. Sounds like home from home."

"Home is right."

The cabin was far more comfortable than Landon had expected. Compared with the quarters on board a corvette, and especially compared with his cabin on board the yawl, it was almost a stateroom. It was separate from the rest of the crew's quarters, opening straight on to the open deck just under the poop. The approach to it was thus sheltered overhead, and it was high enough above the waterline to be clear of any but the heaviest of seas.

The two bunks were placed, one above the other, against the inner bulkhead, with two wardrobes and a settee on the opposite side. At the end of the cabin farthest from the door was a small table fixed to the bulkhead, while under the lower bunk were two capacious drawers. A porthole above the settee was even supplied with a print curtain on a brass rail.

"I didn't think it would be as good as this," Landon said. "You told me it might be tough, but this looks pretty soft."

"I wasn't referring to the quarters," Green said. "I was thinking about the company. Tankers usually have good living, so I've found. Not like some tramps or coasters where the accommodation is real fo'c's'le stuff." He tested the mattress on the lower bunk, thrusting his fist into it. "You fussy about top or bottom?"

Landon shook his head. "I don't care two pins which I have."

"Now there's a funny thing," Green said. "I do. I like the top." He grinned a little sheepishly. "Call it superstition if you like, but I reckon it's unlucky for me to sleep in a bottom bunk. The only time I was torpedoed I had a bottom bunk; same thing when I caught malaria on shore leave in some stinking West African port. It's the same with cards

— never any luck if I'm sleeping in a lower. I reckon if I ever get drowned it'll be because some lousy bastard done me out of the top bunk."

"I shouldn't like to be held responsible for your death," Landon said. "You can do the climbing. Your legs are longer than mine anyway; it'll be easier for you."

He began to unpack his kit. Even with what he had bought that morning it was not extensive. The wardrobe and the drawer swallowed it with ease. He took the new sheath-knife from his bag and slipped the sheath on to his belt, sliding it round to the back of his waist, sailor fashion. The knife had a bone handle and a long, thin blade, pointed at the end. Somehow the very feel of it in the small of his back gave him confidence. With a knife a man was not completely unarmed.

Green said casually, not looking at Landon, busy with his own gear: "You and me, Harvey boy, we travel light. I was never the one to gather much moss. Nor you neither by the look of things. You got business in New York, maybe."

"Yes," Landon said. "Business."

Green was not put off by the curt answer. He was folding a blue roll-neck jersey, very slowly and carefully, as if he had all the time in the world for that particular job. "Me, I'd say it was pretty important business, too, if a man would go as far as to kill you just to stop you doing it. That's what I'd call going to extreme lengths."

For a moment Landon felt the anger rising in him under this probing. Jonas Green was inquisitive; he was asking for information. And what in hell had it got to do with him? It was none of his business. He, Landon, was not asking Green about his troubles; why should he tell the fellow about his?

Then he relaxed. After all, he owed something to Green: the chance of getting away from Buenos Aires. It if had not been for Green he might still have been looking around for a ship, trying perhaps to stow away on board a liner — a risky business even with the best of luck; he might still have been looking over his shoulder at a shuffling, lop-sided man in a blue suit. Oh, yes; he had much to thank Green for.

He slapped his cabin-mate on the shoulder, the black mood gone from him. "I'll tell you some day. Not now."

Green said: "Don't think I'm inquisitive — "

"But I do think so. It doesn't matter."

Green pushed his drawer shut and stood up. He seemed to be about to deny the charge, but at that moment there was an interruption. The door swung open, and a man stood framed in the opening.

He was not a tall man — probably not more than five feet six — but he was so massively built that he seemed to fill the doorway like a plug. He was made after the pattern of an ape: short, thick neck, barrel chest, arms abnormally long, legs short and slightly bowed. His head was shaved and brown as a new football; his brows overshadowed pale-blue eyes, very quick and wary; and on each cheek were horizontal scars so symmetrically placed, one below another, that it seemed they must have been purposely cut in the flesh, either for ornament, as some primitive tribesman might have done, or with the object of torture. Whatever their origin, they did nothing to improve the appearance of a face already made sufficiently unattractive by a broken nose and a thick-lipped cruel mouth.

"You, new men? English, huh?"

He spoke thickly and slowly, as if the words were being ground out of some mill situated in either his belly or his throat. His hands, battered and filthy, were rubbing up and down on the blue dungaree trousers stretched tightly across his muscular thighs. One might have supposed that the hands could not bear to be idle even for a moment, that they had to be doing something, no matter what. They made a continuous smooth, slithering noise that was like a background to the words.

"That's right," Landon said. "We're just moving in."

"Goot — goot. Now you move in, you come an' vork. Plenty blutty vork to do. You come now — pronto."

"Who are you?" Green asked; but Landon was sure he knew the answer to that question even before the man in the doorway replied.

"Me!" He gave a brief, harsh laugh that seemed to come clanging up from his thick belly like the beat of a gong. "Schmidt — Hermann Schmidt — bosun." He lifted one of his battered, dirty hands and thumped himself on the chest. "Ven I tell you do sometings you do sometings fast, pronto, see? No back talkings, no asking vy this, vy that. You do jobs blutty pronto. Savvy?"

Green nodded, staring at the bosun. "Savvy."

"Goot. That you unnerstand. You vant no trouble, you be goot boys. You ask trouble, you get it — plenty. This ship not playground, it vorkhouse." He laughed again, rumbling in appreciation of his own exquisite wit, the horizontal scars on his cheeks moving closer together like the folds of a squeezed accordion, his blue pig-eyes almost disappearing behind the cheek-bones and the overhanging brows. Then, as suddenly as it had started, the laugh ceased.

"Names?"

They gave him their names, and the smooth brown head nodded, jerking on the thick neck as if it had been mounted on rubber.

"Right. You come now. Vork."

He turned away from the door and went stamping off on his short, bowed legs, his long arms swinging at his sides. It seemed that in a moment he might have swung himself up into the rigging, hanging on with hands and feet as his primitive ancestors had done.

Green and Landon followed him.

# 10

## Beyond The Plate

THE crew of the *Gloria del Mar* was a mixture of nationalities and colours, each man with his secrets, each man a mystery to his shipmates. There were hard cases among them, men with whom it was advisable to deal warily, not provoking anger or resentment. Landon, with one object in view — to reach New York, deliver his letter, and receive the five thousand dollars, from Mr Delgado — was not looking for trouble. He trod softly in the mess and at work, trying to arouse no enmity.

The German bosun, Schmidt, was suited to the men he had to handle. A weakling would have been useless; these were men who understood one language only — the language of brutality. And that Hermann Schmidt could speak to perfection.

There was an Irishman in the crew, Danny McNulty, an oldish wizened man who always carried a little wooden cross suspended from his stringy neck by a thin brass chain, perhaps in the hope that, despite a lifetime of sin, the church might in the end save his soul from eternal damnation. He knew something of Schmidt's history, and related it to Jonas Green. Schmidt, it appeared, had once been a Nazi; he had in fact been one of Roehm's men, and the scars on his cheeks had been imprinted during some strange and rather bestial initiation ceremony. When Roehm fell from Hitler's favour and was savagely murdered along with many of his adherents Schmidt had the good fortune to escape to Mexico, where he interested himself in various illegal activities before taking to the sea for the sake of his health.

"He used to crack a whip once," McNulty said. "He was one of Roehm's butchers. When he's drunk he talks. He's still proud of what he did. He calls them 'the goot old days.' Good for him maybe; but not so good for the ones that felt the whip on their backs.

178

"A nice boy to have around the house," Green said. "Pretty, too."

"Sure, he's the nice boy — the sort you'd like to take home to your dear old mother." McNulty cackled like a hen telling the world about its egg. "You want to watch your step with him. Upset any of the rest of the crowd if you must, but keep off Mister Schmidt's corns. That's a tip."

"I wasn't thinking of making trouble with him."

"You don't want to. But he's the sort who goes around looking for it — especially when he's taken a drop. He's strong, too, strong as a gorilla. I believe he could crush a man to death in those two arms of his, sure I do."

"I'll watch my step," Green said.

They were hot days in Buenos Aires. The air where the *Gloria del Mar* lay in dock was like a heavy blanket soaked in oil. A shimmer of heat rose from the sluggish water; the iron decks were hot underfoot like the top of a cooking-stove. And the thick, hoarse voice of the bosun seemed to be everywhere, driving the crew to work.

179

"I shall be glad when we get to sea," Landon said. "This place stinks."

He was feeling jumpy, too. He wanted to see the mooring-ropes cast off, a stretch of water opening between the ship and the shore. These days of waiting irked him. He wondered what was causing the delay. Perhaps even now the crew was not complete. Meanwhile the sun poured its heat into the dock, like a crucible tipping out its load of molten metal. And in the heat Schmidt drove his men, the sweat dripping from his shaven head and hanging like beads of oil on the ladders of his facial scars.

Over the side, sitting on a board suspended on two ropes, Landon chipped and scraped at the flaking paintwork of the riveted plates of the ship, and next to his skin he could feel the letter that he was to deliver personally into the hand of Mr Delgado. He had wrapped it in a piece of oilcloth to protect it from sweat and sea-water, and he kept it with him always, never allowing it away from his person. If he were to lose it he would lose his five thousand dollars, and without the dollars what would there be for him in

New York? He would not even be able to go to Gloria Swindon — not penniless, as a beggar. Perhaps he would be a fool to go to her, anyway; perhaps she had never really meant that he should go, had looked upon him merely as part of her South American adventure, not as some one who might come to life again in the more matter-of-fact atmosphere of the United States.

Angered at the thought, he beat violently upon the steel plate in front of him with the chipping-hammer.

"You hit it like that," Green said, "and you won't just take the rust off; you'll go clean through into the tank. What's biting you?"

"It's this damned heat," Landon said. "Why don't they get us moving?"

"All in good time, boy, all in good time. Things can't be hurried by the likes of you and me. Besides, you know the old saying — more days, more dollars."

"They can keep the dollars. I want to get away."

Green whistled softly. "You are in a hurry, aren't you? But keep a curb on yourself. It don't do to get excited. Bad for the blood pressure."

Landon knew that Green was right. You had to keep calm; no good ever came from losing patience. But the heat was oppressive; even his hands were running with sweat. He struck another blow at the flaking paintwork, and the hammer slipped from his hand, to fall with a gentle *plop* into the oily, garbage-strewn water below him.

"Now you're going to have trouble with Mister flaming Schmidt," Green said gloomily. "He'll be glad of the chance to take a bite out of your ear."

"To hell with Schmidt," Landon said. But he was angry with himself for dropping the hammer and giving the bosun an excuse to swear at him. When fellows of that sort swore at him he was tempted to answer in the same fashion, and if he did that there would just be more trouble. And trouble was what he simply did not want. He had to take it easy. Very soon now the ship would be putting to sea and his worries would be over.

Schmidt noticed the loss of the chipping-hammer when tools were returned to him at the end of the day's work. He bawled Landon out, as Green had predicted.

"You think tools made for you to drop in damn vater, hey? You one Gott damn clumsy sailor. By Gott, I see better ones in girl's school, in kindergarten. You smarten up pronto — else trouble, big trouble. Now you get to hell out of here before I make you sorry. Move!"

Landon took it all without a word, inwardly aflame with resentment and anger because this damned, bullet-headed Nazi thug should be able to speak to him in such terms. He held himself under control, resisting the urge to lash back at Schmidt with tongue and fist, and waited for the bosun to expend his insults. Then he walked away to his own cabin.

Green complimented him. "You took it well. I didn't think you'd be able to keep your temper. I don't know whether I could have done."

Landon wondered whether there was just a hint of sarcasm in Green's voice. He answered savagely: "I feel like dirt. He'd better not try it too often."

"Then you'd better not give him the excuse."

When the evening came it was not cool. Mosquitoes hummed in the sultry air, drawn to the ship's lights, their bites bringing up irritations in the flesh. Landon lounged on the poop, his shirt open and hanging loose, exposing the scar on his belly.

Green, standing beside him, whistled softly, his head wagging. "Well, I'll say you took something there. No wonder you get the pains sometimes. How did it happen?"

"Never mind that," Landon said. He did not wish to live it over again even in recollection — the tearing, slicing passage of the steel, the rough first aid, the transference to a destroyer, the probing of splinters, the weeks and months of slow recovery. Whenever he saw the scar it reminded him; when the pain racked him it told him once again what it had been like the first time.

Over the city of Buenos Aires was a glow of light, dimming the stars. From dozens of tango bands came music closer and louder than the music of spheres

184

— pulsating, rhythmic dances to set the fires of youth alight. But Landon, leaning on the rail of the *Gloria del Mar*, did not hear the music. He looked towards the city, thinking only of a man with a drooping lip and a shuffling step — a killer.

"To-morrow," Green said softly. "To-morrow we shall be on our way."

In the water under the stern of the ship a lamp was reflected. He dropped a five-centavo piece into the watery lamp, and it shattered into a thousand shivering splinters of light.

"For luck," he said.

Landon answered, speaking half to himself: "I'll need that luck."

★ ★ ★

The tugs came early, moving the vessel out on to the broad back of the river Plate. Her propeller began to turn, and the water foamed up, yellow with mud, swilling round the rudder. A wind came off the sea, gentle and warm, but fresh and sweet-smelling after the hot odours of the land. Sea-birds floated above the masts, flapping lazy wings; white birds were silhouetted against the empty blue of the sky. And from the jack-staff streamed and fluttered the red, white, and blue, starred and quartered flag of Panama.

They were away. The ties binding the vessel to the land had been cast off, and they were away. The river would float them down to the sea, and the sea would float them northward. And northward lay New York and Mr Delgado, and five thousand dollars, and Gloria Swindon.

Landon, watching the city falling astern and the river widening to the sea, was pleased. He felt the easing of that tension which had been in him for days; he had cleared the last big fence, and ahead lay nothing but plain sailing.

"Hey, you there! Vot in hell you think you do?" It was the thick, grating voice of Schmidt, the bosun, calling him rudely back from visions of the future to the realities of the present. "You stand an' dream ven there is jobs to do. Damn you! Vot you think you paid for? Move!"

Landon moved. Schmidt sent him down into the locker, where the mooring-ropes were stowed aft. Now that the ship

186

was moving away from the land her decks were being cleared of all the litter and garbage that had descended on them during the time in dock, and the ropes had to be stowed out of the way. An electric winch was turning, rolling the great python-thick cables over its drum and down into the locker. And as they came down, snaking and flailing, Landon and Paddy McNulty had to lay them in place, coiling them neatly in the narrow space of the locker.

It was oven-hot within the steel walls; the sweat poured from them, and the ropes seemed endless. Schmidt peered down through the hatch, snarling if anything went wrong.

"Ach! Sailors! Gott's blutt! A blutty dog could spew up better men on a meal of sauerkraut an' sausage."

Already Landon was hating Schmidt. It was not difficult to imagine him in the rôle of one of Roehm's storm troopers, torturing Jews, Communists, anyone he could lay his hands on — anyone who happened to be weak and defenceless.

"He used to strangle women prisoners," McNulty had once confided to Landon, lowering his voice as if in fear that Schmidt might be listening. "After he'd had his way with them he'd strangle them, either with a cord or with his bare hands. He'll boast about it when he's in liquor. You've seen his hands. He'll demonstrate just how it was done when he's in the mood. 'Like so,' he says. 'Press, press, press.' He says it was like having life in your hands. He loved it."

"You don't think he was lying — spinning a yarn to impress people when the drink was in him?"

"Not a chance of it. When he's drunk, that's when he really tells the truth. You can't trust him any other time."

"The filthy swine!"

"Ah, he's a swine all right, but you don't want to tell him so. He's not just in love with you as it is; he's got a grudge against the English. If you really want to get his dander up ask him who won the War."

"I don't want to get him riled," Landon said. "I'm looking for a quiet life."

"You came to the wrong ship," McNulty said.

Landon wondered whether, try to

control himself though he might, a time would perhaps come when Hermann Schmidt would goad him into retaliation. There were limits to what a man of spirit could take, and Schmidt might push him beyond those limits. But it would be unfortunate, for Landon truly did not want trouble. Things were going well. Soon they would be dropping the pilot; soon Montevideo would be drifting away on the port quarter, and the open sea would lie ahead. Then all the power of the Central Republic and all its agents could not touch him; he would be beyond their influence. He had been fortunate in running into Jonas Green; perhaps Green was a talisman. It would have been better if there had been a different bosun on board the *Gloria del Mar*, but you could not have it all ways.

The end of the last mooring-rope came slapping down into the locker. Landon twisted it round on top of the coil and leaned back against the steel bulkhead, panting from his labours, wiping the sweat from his face.

"Paddy," he said, "I could do with a drink — a long, cold drink."

Then he heard Schmidt's voice again. "Vot you do down there? You think you finish vork, hey? You come up here damn quick — pronto. I find you jobs to do. Come!"

Landon and McNulty climbed out of the locker. The bosun was waiting for them, his battered hands swinging loosely at his sides. Landon, remembering what McNulty had said, could well imagine those hands strangling the life out of a woman, and Schmidt taking a delight in the act.

"You two — for'ard now. Double quick!"

He went in front of them, rolling slightly on his bowed, stumpy legs, and they followed him along the cat-walk, with the muddy river-water sliding past on either side and the white sea-birds fluttering above the ship like ghosts.

But even Schmidt could not keep them at work for ever. They were slaves to the ship, but there were hours that were their own — evening hours when, if they were not on watch and if it was not their trick at the wheel, they could be idle, could lounge on the deck and

190

find delight in the cooler air coming off the sea, drying the sweat from their tired bodies.

It was evening on the day the *Gloria del Mar* had sailed from Buenos Aires, and Landon was leaning on the rails at the end of the after cat-walk. He was looking towards the bridge when a man came out of the midships accommodation and paused for a moment, gazing aft towards the crew's quarters.

He was wearing a white steward's jacket with silver buttons, fastened high at the neck, and blue trousers. The light was good, and Landon could see him clearly. The ship was meeting a swell, and the cat-walk was tilting first one way and then the other, so that Landon and the steward were like two men standing at opposite ends of a long see-saw. For perhaps a minute they stared at each other across the see-saw; then the steward turned and disappeared through the door-way out of which he had come.

But Landon had recognized him as surely as if they had been standing face to face without a foot of space to separate them. It was the man with the drooping lip and the dragging step, the man who had worn a blue suit — the killer.

# 11

## No Refuge

SO even the ship was to be no refuge. Landon did not waste time in wondering how his pursuer had trailed him; the important point was that he had done so. Landon had thought at first that the man was a tyro, clumsy at his job, perhaps not greatly to be feared. He had good reason since then to alter his opinion. This man was as dangerous as he was skilled.

In the few days that the *Gloria del Mar* had lain idle in her berth he had succeeded in tracing Landon to the ship and he had also managed to get himself taken on as a steward. Perhaps he had used rather more than verbal persuasion on that sleek, smooth chief steward, Castro. Whatever his methods, he had succeeded. Here he was firmly established in a position of advantage, and for Landon the ship was no longer a refuge but a trap. Now he could not escape; constant vigilance must be his only defence. And how could one be for ever vigilant on board a ship at sea?

He felt that the time had come to take Green fully into his confidence. Green was the only one he could look to for help, and he might need help badly. He had no trust in the ship's officers. If he went to Captain Sharpe with his tale about the steward he would be laughed at. True, Sharpe was an Englishman, one of Landon's own countrymen, but in the case of such a man that might mean little. As for the other officers, they were not English and not of a kind to be looked to for help.

Green, when told, said: "You're quite sure this is the man who shot at you in B.A.? You aren't making a mistake? Perhaps the two just look alike."

"There couldn't be two like him," Landon said with conviction. "I'm making no mistake."

"That letter you're carrying must be damned important if they'll go to these lengths to prevent it reaching its destination."

"To these people," Landon said, "revolutions are the most important things in life. That letter may mean the difference between success and failure for the Vargas faction. Romero's government will go all out to make sure it isn't delivered to Delgado. I've no doubt this killer is being well paid for his trouble."

Green lit a cigarette, staring at Landon, his beaked nose with its bony ridge thrust forward like the prow of a boat. "And what do you stand to gain — supposing you get through?"

"Five thousand dollars."

Green took the cigarette out of his mouth and gave a long whistle. "As much as that? It's a nice fat slab of dough. No wonder you were keen to get out of B.A."

Landon sensed that Green still had doubts — not perhaps about the general truth of the story, but about the new steward. In that particular he seemed to think that Landon might be deluding himself. But after he had a talk with Paddy McNulty he was inclined to change his opinion.

"Paddy's the boy for ferreting out information. I asked him if he's seen a new steward with a dragging foot and a slumped shoulder, and he said he had. He saw him as soon as he came on board, just a little while before we sailed. He was wearing a blue suit then and carrying one of those soft-topped suitcases. Castro met him at the gangway, and McNulty heard him say something in Spanish, and then Castro took hold of this new feller's arm and took him inside. They looked pretty matey, as if that wasn't the first time they'd met each other, not by a long chalk."

"Did Paddy find out the bastard's name?"

"He did that too — trust Paddy. The man's a Pole — name of Henryk Golbek. He speaks Spanish, but no English. Can't get any more information than that. But I'd say he was your man all right."

"He's a killer," Landon said. "Have you seen his eyes?"

"I haven't been close to him," Green said. "He's nothing to write home about even at a distance."

"Take a good look when you get the

chance. You'll see what I mean. To that sort of man killing could be just a job like any other, no different from laying bricks or adding up a column of figures."

Shortly afterwards they both had an opportunity of seeing Golbek at close quarters. He was in the storeroom when they went to collect their rations. When Landon held out his container for the steward to pour into it the measured quantity of coffee their eyes met. In Golbek's cold, dead eyes there was no hint of recognition; there was no colour in his muddy face. But Landon knew there could not be two Golbeks; he detected the odour of cheap scent, like the stuff sometimes sprayed in low-class cinemas, and again he experienced that feeling of revulsion that had come over him when he had gripped the man's arm in the Buenos Aires street.

He said in Spanish: "I know you. We have met before."

The man's face was expressionless. "I do not think so. I cannot recall any meeting."

It was the first time that Landon had heard his voice. It came as a surprise, almost with the shock of a blow. It might have been a woman's voice — soft, unbroken, with the faintest suspicion of a lisp, pedantically giving to each word its full value. He finished doling out the coffee and fetched Landon's ration of sugar.

"I am new to this ship. How could we have met before?"

Landon wondered whether the fellow were laughing at him. But there was no hint of laughter in the soft, lisping voice, no trace of a smile on the bloodless face.

"It was not on board ship that we met."

"No? Then where could it have been?"

"You know damn well — "

It was Castro, the chief steward, who ended the exchange with his smooth, oily voice. "Take your stores and go, please. Do not block the way for others."

Landon left the storeroom and went back across the cat-walk to his own quarters, angry with himself. To be afraid of that wretched, subhuman creature with the lisping, woman's voice was despicable. Was he afraid? He asked himself the question bluntly. With blunt honesty he had to admit that to a certain extent he was. Only a fool would be without fear in such a situation. Look at the facts: this man, Golbek, wished to kill him; they were together on board a ship at sea; there would be a hundred opportunities to gratify that wish. Therefore Landon could not avoid being afraid; yet, knowing what a miserable creature it was that had made him so, he was angry also.

Green came into the cabin a few minutes later.

"You had a look at Golbek's eyes?" Landon asked.

Green nodded. "I know what you mean now. You were talking to him. Hasn't he the lovely sweet voice? What was he saying?"

"He assured me I was mistaken if I supposed we had met. He had never seen me before."

"You still think he's your man?"

"I haven't the faintest shred of a doubt about it. Did you smell that muck he uses?"

"The 'Night of Love' stuff? Couldn't miss it."

"He reeked of that in Buenos Aires. It clinches the matter."

"He's a sweet little customer," Green said. "What do we do? Throw him overboard?"

"It might save a lot of trouble."

★ ★ ★

Golbek did not waste time in making the first move. On the evening of the second day out from Buenos Aires Landon went to his cabin and found Green sniffing the air. Green turned as Landon came in and gave him a half-humorous quizzical look.

"Smells like there's been a tart in here. You taken to using scent, Harvey boy?"

Landon caught a whiff of it then — not strong, but unmistakable.

He said: "Golbek's been in here."

Green snapped his fingers. "Of course, I knew I'd smelt that stuff before. He's got a nerve, coming in here. Do you think he was looking for you?"

"I think he was looking for this letter," Landon said, smacking his pocket. "Maybe he thought I would leave it in the cabin ready for him to pick up."

He moved to his bunk and looked at the blankets. They were not as tidily arranged as they had been when he left the cabin.

"Well, he's had his search in vain. I wonder what his next move will be. I must say your suggestion about flinging him over the side begins to look more attractive. After all, that's where all the garbage should go."

"Are you serious?" Green asked.

There was no smile twitching the corners of Landon's thin-lipped mouth. "I may have had the better part of my life," he said, "but I'd be reluctant to throw the rest of it away. I may be biased, but I happen to think it's worth a whole lot more than our dear friend Golbek's. Perhaps he'd better watch his step too."

But as the ship ploughed her way northward, towards the jutting elbow of South America, it was from Schmidt that the trouble came.

The crew's mess was a long, narrow room with a table, also long and narrow, down the middle, and chairs on either side. There was an electric water heater, a sink, and lockers for storing crockery and other utensils. A loudspeaker, screwed to one of the bulkheads, relayed occasional news bulletins and music from the ship's radio receiver. Here, in the evenings, gambling schools collected, and money, hard earned by long hours of labour and discomfort, was thrown away in an instant on the turn of a card.

Jonas Green was a born gambler, and so was Paddy McNulty; but this was a form of amusement that held no attraction for Landon. Risking money on the chance of a card or the uncertain running of a horse did not interest him. It was not that he had any puritanical feelings of disapproval; it was simply that the gambler's pastimes produced in him not excitement but boredom. He would sometimes watch the others, but he took no hand himself.

Hermann Schmidt, like Green and McNulty and most of the others in the crew, was a gambler, heart and soul. If it had not been so he would never have demeaned himself by coming into the seamen's mess and playing cards with those same men whom all day he goaded with the venom of his tongue. For the sake of poker he swallowed his pride and sat among the crew like any ordinary seaman.

"Cards is my pleasure. I love cards like they is precious jewels. Deal them round."

He was not a very popular guest, but it would have been impolitic to attempt to exclude him. To offend the bosun was not the way to make life pleasant for oneself. Yet to win his money was dangerous also, and thus the players were in a dilemma: they did not wish to lose, but they were wary of winning. Only the reckless took Schmidt's money. When he was backing his hand most of the others took care to fall out fairly quickly.

McNulty was one of the reckless ones. Perhaps it was that he could not bear to throw away good hands, to lose when the luck was running strongly in his favour — even to Schmidt. Perhaps he felt that it would be almost sacrilegious to spurn the favours of fortune.

Usually he tried to join a different school from that in which the bosun was engaged, but this was not always possible. It was on the third evening out from Buenos Aires when the unfortunate combination of circumstances occurred: McNulty was involved already in a poker game when Schmidt came into the mess-room. Schmidt did not wait to be invited; he sat down and took a hand. "I try my luck, no?"

No one had the hardihood to object. McNulty's wizened body seemed to shrink a little further, but he said nothing. Landon lit himself a cigarette and prepared to watch the fun, if it could be called fun when Schmidt was taking the seamen's money.

But from the outset the cards ran for the Irishman; full houses, fours, even the straight flush came to him, while the best that Schmidt could put against this phenomenal run of luck were occasional straights or threes. Schmidt bluffed, but it was no use, for McNulty, flinging aside all discretion in the excitement of his winning hands, called the bluff again and again. Schmidt's breathing became heavy, and a deep flush crept up his thick neck, up to the roots of his shaven hair. This was an experience to which he was not accustomed, and he was not enjoying it. Rage was boiling up in him as McNulty took his money. His blue pig-eyes seemed to withdraw under his heavy brows, staring out balefully.

McNulty should have read the warning signs, should have taken care; but he was blinded by his luck. Hands like these came once in a lifetime; to ask him not to make use of them would have been demanding the impossible.

Once more the cards were dealt, the bets were made; one by one the players retired until only McNulty and Schmidt were left in. Schmidt was breathing like a man who has just finished a hard race; the sweat was standing out on his forehead in big drops that gleamed under the mess-room lights.

Green nudged McNulty with his elbow. "Throw in, you damned fool," he whispered. He could see that Schmidt was nearing the limit of his self-control, that in a moment something would have to break.

But McNulty was deaf to reason or caution; he was riding on a flood-tide of success and he meant to ride it for all it was worth. He matched Schmidt's stake and laid his cards on the table with an air of triumph that made Green wince. They were the ten, Jack, Queen, King and Ace of Spades — an unbeatable straight flush, the hand of a lifetime.

"There now; isn't that a beauty?" he said. He was grinning foolishly, like a man half drunk. "Sure, I never saw anything so lovely. They're the sweet cards, the darlin' cards — "

He might have said more, but Schmidt, with one swift movement of his arms, swept the cards and the money from the table. He flung his chair back and stood up, panting.

"You damn *schwein*! You blutty cheat! You cheat all blutty time. I make you vish you were dead. I make you vish you never been born."

He reached across the table and picked up McNulty as easily as if he had been picking up a child. He dragged him across the table, clamped his long, ape-like arms about the Irishman's puny chest, and began to squeeze.

McNulty, scared out of his complacency,

yelled: "I didn't cheat. It was just the way the cards were running. I swear I didn't — "

"Liar! Damn, blutty liar! I teach you now one goot lesson. I think you never cheat no more."

The pressure on the arms increased. McNulty began to whimper. The other men in the mess-room were silent, watching, interested spectators of this demonstration of Schmidt's muscular strength, perhaps enjoying the exhibition of primitive torture. No one spoke; the only sounds were the beat of the ship's diesel engines, the creak of timbers as she rolled, McNulty whimpering, and the hard, laboured breathing of Hermann Schmidt. They waited for the sound of McNulty's ribs cracking.

McNulty had told Green that he believed Schmidt could crush a man to death with his two arms; now he was in a position to test the truth of that contention. He was locked against the great barrel chest of the bosun, encircled by arms like steel hoops, with his own arms clamped firmly at his sides. He was helpless and he was afraid. His ribs would be crushed in like a wicker basket. He could scarcely breathe. He looked appealingly round the mess-room and saw no hand raised to help him, only gloating faces, men enjoying the spectacle of his agony.

Schmidt took a deep breath and tightened his grip. McNulty began to scream — a thin, miserable scream of fear and anguish, like that of an animal caught in a trap.

It had become more than Landon could stand. His voice seemed to cut through the tension like a knife slicing a stretched cord.

"That's enough. Let him go."

Schmidt was so surprised that his grip on McNulty slackened a little. He glared at Landon.

"Vot you say?"

"I said let him go. What do you think you're doing? Do you want to kill him?"

"You keep your nose out," Schmidt said. "You mind your own blutty business, or maybe you get hurt too. This *schwein* cheat. I teach him one goot lesson. You keep out."

The other men looked from Schmidt to Landon, sensing the conflict of wills, even though many of them could not understand the words. Landon's voice was incisive, still cutting like a knife.

"Eyewash! He didn't cheat. If you knew more about poker you might be able to win straight. When you win it's because the others are too damned yellow to stop you."

He was purposely goading Schmidt now in order to save McNulty from further torture. He had to bring Schmidt's anger to bear against himself. And in that he was successful. Schmidt's grip relaxed, and McNulty slipped from his arms. He crawled to a chair and sat there, gasping for breath, feeling his ribs and groaning.

Schmidt said hoarsely: "You say that to me! You say I not know poker!"

"You couldn't beat a half-witted Chinaman," Landon said.

Schmidt's face was purple, the colour coming in blotches like a disease. "Gott's blutt! I teach you manners. I teach you — " He hurled himself round the end of the table, his hands lifted to grab Landon as they had grabbed McNulty.

"You damn English bastard. I teach you sometings. I make you squeal now."

Landon did not move away. He slipped his knife out of its sheath and held it in front of him, the point aimed unwaveringly at Schmidt's belly.

"You want this in your guts? If so, come on." There was no passion in his voice; it was ice-cold, calm, unemphatic, almost conversational. Schmidt looked into his eyes, and halted, uncertain, his hands still thrust forward a little way in front of him, the scarred fingers opening and closing, as though eager to be at Landon's throat and waiting only for the order.

"So — a knife — "

He trembled, not with fear, but with the suppressed power of his anger. He wanted to rush at Landon, to seize and savage him; but the knife made him halt. He had no wish for six inches of steel in his belly, and he knew that the man standing in front of him would not hesitate to thrust home.

"A damn knife. You think that fair play?"

"I'm not interested in fair play,"

210

Landon said. "But I am interested in keeping your hands off my skin. Understand?"

The sound of McNulty's groaning and the sound of Schmidt's breathing seemed to fill the mess-room. No man moved; they were all fearful of breaking the tension. Time itself seemed to have come to rest, to be waiting — as these men were waiting, breathless.

Then Schmidt laughed. There was something forced about it, but it was a laugh, and had to be taken as such.

"Put the knife avay. Put it avay. Vot sense spilling blutt, hey? You there, Jonas — deal the cards. Ve play some more. Maybe I vin your money; maybe you vin mine. Let us play."

He sat down heavily. Landon slipped the knife back into its sheath. The men began to chatter. The tension was broken.

But Schmidt had been taken down, and it was Landon who had taken him down — in the presence of the whole mess. He would not forget.

# 12

## In the Tank

"FOR a man who's supposed to be looking for a quiet life, Harvey boy," Green said as he rolled himself a cigarette before climbing into his bunk, "you seem to have a natural genius for sticking your neck out. I warned you not to tread on Mister Schmidt's corns, and what do you do? You jump all over them with hobnailed boots. He'll be after your blood now, and no mistake. You took him off his high and mighty perch, a thing he won't be able to stomach."

"He went too far. Another minute and he'd have done that poor little devil some real injury. I couldn't stand by and watch that happen."

"No?" Green licked the cigarette-paper and smoothed it down with his long, thin fingers. "Plenty of others could. You wouldn't have found anyone

212

else interfering."

"Not you?"

"I look out for number one. I don't know just how long I may be aboard this ship, and while I'm here I want to live in as much comfort as possible. I don't want trouble with no whip-man bosun. Paddy was a fool, anyway; he asked for what he got. If you play cards with Schmidt you have to let him win; that's one of the rules of the game. You wouldn't catch me taking his money — at least, not much of it."

"Perhaps I'm not built the same way as everybody else," Landon said. "Torture just happens to stick in my gullet, that's all. Besides, if this damned bosun had his deserts he'd probably be swinging at the end of a hangman's rope."

"Maybe he would; but things don't always turn out the way they should in this world. You have to make the best of them as they are."

"That may be your philosophy. I have different ideas."

Nevertheless, he knew that he had been forced into making a false move. He had had enough to contend with

213

already, looking out for Golbek, without incurring Schmidt's enmity. Of the two, however, he believed that Schmidt was the less dangerous, even though he could probably have smashed half a dozen men like Golbek with his bare hands. Schmidt was the rhinoceros charging with blind fury, but Golbek was the adder biting with poisoned fangs.

"You watch out all the same," Green said. He put one foot on the rail of the lower bunk and vaulted agilely into the top one, the cigarette between his lips. "You want that five thousand dollars, don't you? Well, boy, if I was in your shoes I'd feel like settling for a thousand right now — if it was offered."

* * *

Landon finished his trick at the wheel at the end of the middle watch — four o'clock in the morning. The moon was up, and as he walked back across the cat-walk towards the crew's quarters he could see it glinting palely on the wash on either side of the ship. He could hear the *rush-rush-rush*-ing sound of the water

214

as it flowed past, like a torrent foaming over rapids. The ship was north of the Tropic of Capricorn now and pressing on towards Rio Grande do Norte, towards the point where she would alter course to westward.

The days were passing, and still Golbek had made no further move. Landon had been watchful, treading warily; but there were times when it was not possible to guard oneself. Now, for instance, walking across the cat-walk, he was in the full light of the moon. A man could have waited in the shadow of the midships accommodation and shot him down with ease.

What was Golbek waiting for? Did he want to lull his victim into a feeling of security before he acted? There was time and to spare. He knew that Landon could not slip away; while it was at sea the ship was a prison more secure than any of the gaols in the Central Republic. Golbek could bide his time.

Landon came to the end of the cat-walk and thought he saw a shadow move at the corner of the superstructure on the starboard side. It seemed to him as though a man had peered out and then withdrawn himself.

Landon went across to the port rails, moving fast. He turned the angle of the housing on that side and came round the stern, treading softly, cat-like, in rubber-soled shoes. If the shadow had in fact been Golbek he would catch him in the rear; he would wring the fellow's filthy neck. Perhaps this was the opportunity he had been waiting for, the chance to throw Golbek overboard. Who would know? If he were rid of Golbek he would be rid of the constant feeling of apprehension, the continual fear of a knife or a bullet in the back.

He came softly, warily from the stern, under the shelter of the poop-deck, avoiding the bollards and ventilator shafts. He could hear the *tonk-tonk-tonk* of the diesel exhaust coming from the funnel and the beat of the propeller blades, just breaking the surface of the water on the top part of their revolution. He kept in close to the deckhouse wall, in the shadow.

But he found no one; not even a shadow of a man. Perhaps he had imagined seeing one. Was he to be tricked now by his own senses? He cursed softly, looking towards the bridge across the dark chasm of the main deck, wondering whether there had really been anyone. He could see no one now, no one walking back along the cat-walk. Perhaps he had imagined it. And yet there were so many corners in which a man might hide. Who could tell?

He went into his cabin and kicked off his shoes. He stretched himself out on his bunk, not troubling to undress. He lit a cigarette and began to smoke, listening to the whirring of the electric fan and the thump of the diesels, and trying to reckon in his head how many more days would have to pass before they reached Philadelphia.

Green stirred in the bunk above, muttering in his sleep. Landon stubbed out the butt of the cigarette and lay in the humid darkness, sweating.

\* \* \*

On the following day a gang was set to work cleaning out some of the ship's tanks — those deep, narrow cells that made the vessel like a vast honeycomb, each cell a watertight compartment sealed off from the others by steel bulkheads. Landon and Green were in one party working in a tank midway between the forecastle and the bridge. The water ballast had been pumped out of the tank, and it was their job now to shovel out the rusty sludge that had been deposited at the bottom.

"Nice work," Green said, a streak of rust like a bleeding wound crossing his forehead. "Like being a blooming well-digger."

There were similarities. Standing on the bottom of the tank was rather like being at the bottom of a well, and the iron floor was so thick with the rust that had flaked off the sides or fallen from above that it was possible to imagine oneself to be standing on gritty earth, forgetting for the moment the hundreds of fathoms of sea-water that lay beneath one's feet.

"Don't dig too deep, though," Green said, "or you may let the flood in."

The sound of their shovels echoed

hollowly in the tank as they loaded the sludge into buckets to be drawn up to the hatch far above and emptied over the ship's side. As the bucket went up, swinging, splashes of rusty water slopped over its brim, falling on the men below. They shouted abuse at those above, their voices beating on the sides of the tank. An iron ladder zigzagged up the inner wall, clammy with moisture and stained red with rust. At intervals there were narrow platforms connecting the flights of the ladder, railed for safety. With the ship rolling even slightly the foothold on these slippery platforms was precarious, and if a man were to fall he would be smashed to death on the pipes or the iron floor of the tank.

Landon paused in his shovelling and looked up at the narrow hatch. It looked a long way off — a small square of daylight, an opening letting in the air. But not much fresh air seemed to reach the bottom, for there was a dank, unwholesome smell that matched well the gloomy appearance of that confined space.

Suppose, Landon thought, some one

were to close the lid of that hatch and clamp it down with the men inside. Suppose the pumps started pumping sea-water into the prison.

"A proper trap for drowning rats," he said.

"What's that?" Green asked. "What you blabbering about?"

"I was only thinking that we'd be in a fine mess if anybody with a dislike to us battened us down inside this tank and turned the water on. Couldn't get out, could we?"

Green gave him a queer look. "You think too much. I suppose you fancy Golbek might try that one. Use your loaf; there's too many men down here, and he wouldn't be getting the chance, anyway. You're letting your imagination run away with you. You go on like that and you'll need your head seeing to when we get to Philly."

Landon grinned. "I wasn't really thinking it would happen. But I'm just naturally given to morbid ideas. Hell, these are pleasant surroundings to work in. Just what the doctor ordered for claustrophobics."

220

"Whatever they might be," Green said.

A single electric-light bulb, suspended from the hatch on a length of wire, illuminated the tank, showing the stark, riveted sides and the streaks of rust stretching downward. The bare light cast grotesque shadows, the shadows of men distorted by the swinging lamp and the angles of the bulk-heads. The sound of the shovels and brooms scraping the sludge from the bottom was a harsh accompaniment to the weird ballet movements of their twisting shadows.

"If you find any gold," Green said, "let me know."

"The only one that'll find gold in this ship is the Greek."

Shortly before the end of the morning shift the mate came down into the tank to inspect the work, with the bosun following him. The mate was a tall, saturnine man with an air of great weariness, as though he found the mere act of living a burden almost too heavy to bear. He carried an electric torch, and shone its thin pencil-beam into the inaccessible places under the suction pipes. He found rust, and shook his head sadly, as if he had expected nothing better. He murmured a few words to the bosun, and the bosun nodded vigorously, his brown, shaven head bobbing on the rubbery neck.

Then the mate climbed languidly out of the tank, and Schmidt turned on Landon, glad to find fault, to spit out some of the venom that was in him.

"You think you do goot?" He pointed to the hiding places of rust that the mate's torch had revealed. "You do damn bad. Blutty English! Damn, no-goot English! You get down there, clean that rust out. You vork now ven I tell you. Must I alvays be at your damn heels? Are you goot for nothing?"

He stood watching Landon dragging the sludge out with a broom, gloating over him, exercising his authority for the sake of feeding his damaged self-esteem. Landon had taken him down a peg or two in the mess-room, but here he was master again, and he would exercise that mastery to the full. If only he had had a whip in his hand the picture would have been complete.

Landon did as he was told, saying

nothing. Abuse would not harm him, and as long as Schmidt confined himself to legitimate orders there was no excuse for rebellion. It was unfortunate that he should have antagonized the man when he already had Golbek to deal with, but it could not be helped. The thing now was not to give Schmidt any cause for increased animosity. He was not afraid of the man; he looked upon him simply as a nuisance, a damned nuisance. He detested him also, but that was for what Schmidt had been — and still was — not for anything that he might do.

When work ended for the morning the men climbed the ladders out of the tank, one after another, until only Landon and Schmidt were left below. Schmidt seemed purposely to be waiting, for when Green stood back, giving him the chance to go ahead, Schmidt pushed him to the ladder with a thrust of his long arm. "Go! Vy are you stopping here? Is time for you to go."

Green climbed the ladder, and Schmidt followed slowly, allowing the gap between them to open. Landon came last of all, held back by the slow-moving bosun. At

223

the half-way platform Schmidt halted, breathing heavily, as though the climb had winded him. Landon, looking up, saw Green reach the hatch and climb out of the tank. He came up to the half-way platform and waited for Schmidt to move on.

"Why have you stopped?" he asked. "Is anything wrong?"

Schmidt did not answer. He was hanging on to the guard-rail, breathing very heavily indeed. His head was bowed over his chest. Landon wondered whether he had some kind of heart attack. With a neck like that the fellow might suffer from high blood pressure — probably did. Perhaps the climb up the ladder had been too much for him.

He asked again: "Are you all right, bosun?" And he stepped up on to the platform beside Schmidt.

Schmidt moved very little. A shift of perhaps six inches sideways was sufficient. His shoulder drove against Landon, catching him off balance just as he was taking his right foot from the top rung of the ladder. Landon felt himself falling and grabbed at the handrail. He got his fingers round it, but the rail was slippery with moisture, and he could not keep his grip. His left leg slipped between the rungs of the ladder, and he found the sides of the tank sliding past him as he fell backward.

The electric light flashed across his line of vision like a meteor; he felt a stunning blow on the back of his head and a tearing, wrenching pain in his left ankle and then found that he was hanging on the ladder by one foot, head downward. It was only the fact that his left leg had slipped through between two rungs that had saved him, for the foot had become hooked over a rung and was wedged. If it had not been so he would have fallen straight down to the bottom of the tank and certain death.

He was in pain and he was frightened. He thought his leg must surely be broken and that at any moment it might slip from the ladder and allow him to fall headlong into space. He yelled with fear.

And then he became aware of Schmidt again. Schmidt was leaning over the edge of the platform, one arm hooked round the upright of the handrail, and the other reaching down towards Landon's foot. He was surely going to complete the job now. He was going to disentangle Landon's left foot and let him slide down into the tank.

Landon yelled again, his yells drumming against the rusty sides of the tank. When he paused, choking, he heard Schmidt's voice just above him.

"You blutty English fool! Vy you make that noise? It vill not help you. Keep quiet, damn you!"

Schmidt's hand came down and gripped his left ankle. He could feel Schmidt struggling to release the leg from where it had become wedged in the ladder. The pain almost drove the fear from his mind. Blood was running to his head, drumming in his ears. In his stomach too was the tearing pain that he had had when the shell splinters struck him; it was like being wounded all over again.

He no longer yelled. What was the use? Nothing could save him. He hung limp while Schmidt fumbled and tugged at his leg, sending the waves of agony through his body. He could hear Schmidt's

226

laboured breathing; he could hear him swearing softly to himself. "Gott damn it! Blutt an' hellfire!"

Then suddenly he heard Schmidt shout: "You there — up there! A rope — quick — damn you!"

Another moment and there was a rope slipping round Landon's waist, tightening. Then he was being hauled up. He came the right way up; his leg came free from the ladder; up higher yet; over the rim of the hatch and out on to the open deck, with the sun shining down upon him. The sun was warm, and yet he was shivering, shivering violently and uncontrollably, as if his whole body had been struck with ague. As if through a haze of distance, he heard the voices of men, but the throbbing of blood in his ears mingled with the sound. Then, above all the rest, he heard one voice, thick and hoarse and laughing.

"The blutty fool. He slip on the ladder. If I am not there to help he is dead now. He is damn lucky to be alive; I tell you so. Blutty, clumsy fool! Sailor, bah!"

Landon said nothing. What was there he could say? No one had seen the bosun thrust a shoulder into him. If he told the story it would be only his word against Schmidt's. He might be believed; he might not. In either case the result would be the same, because there had been no witnesses.

"He is not vorth it," Schmidt was saying, "but I save his blutty life. He should thank me, the damn fool."

Damn fool! Yes, that was what he was. He should never have given Schmidt the opportunity to thrust him from the platform; he should have kept a safe distance. Schmidt had purposely waited, purposely allowed the others to go on ahead so that he could make this attempt at murder. It had only been when the others had come running back to gaze down through the hatch that he had changed his line. Now he was setting himself up as a hero, a saver of life.

Landon began to laugh too.

# 13

## Liquid Gold

IT was Jonas Green's stated opinion that Landon was lucky, very lucky indeed.

"If Schmidt pushed you — and I see no reason to doubt that he did — it's a miracle that you're alive to tell the tale. I saw a man fall into one of them tanks once — that was a Yankee tanker in New York in December — in sub-zero temperatures and ice on the ladders. He fell from the top and he didn't bounce. What was left of him we brought up in a canvas cargo sling. I ain't easily upset, but it made me sick as a dog. But you — you catch your leg in the ladder and you don't even break the leg. A couple of days and you'll be fine and dandy once again. You certainly are the lucky man."

Landon's left leg was a mass of bruises

from ankle to knee. A lot of skin had been scraped off on the ladder, and he had a bump on the back of his head. He had been sick, too, vomiting up food and bitter liquid from his wrenched stomach. But that had passed, and Green was right: he was lucky to be alive, for there could be no doubt that Schmidt, with venom in his heart, had meant to kill him.

"Do you think Golbek had a hand in it?" Green asked. "Do you think maybe he bribed Schmidt?"

Landon shook his head. "I don't think so. I don't think there's any love lost between those two, and Golbek is quite capable of doing his own dirty work. No; I'd say this was just something the bosun tried for his own gratification. He couldn't swallow that business over the cards."

"You've got two people to look out for now, then — Golbek and Schmidt. You're not in the healthiest of positions. Not what the insurance companies would call a good risk."

"I don't think Schmidt will try anything more," Landon said. "He's got his own back. He's made me squeal. I think he'll call it a day."

Green laughed. "You certainly squealed all right. We could hear you half a ship's length away. Which was just as well for you, as things panned out."

In the days that followed — hot, sweltering days, as the ship ploughed steadily towards the coast of Venezuela — it appeared that Landon was right, for Schmidt made no further move against him. Indeed, the bosun treated him now with a bluff heartiness that was not altogether unfriendly. True, he still called Landon a 'blutty damn fool Englishman,' but there was no venom in the expression. It was just the kind of thing that sprang naturally to the lips of such a man; it was almost a term of endearment.

Landon wondered whether he could perhaps have been mistaken — whether the incident in the tank had in fact been an accident, caused by a slight roll of the ship throwing Schmidt against him. But he dismissed the idea. It had been deliberate; he was sure of that. And he still believed that if the other men had not been attracted by his yells, had not come back and looked down the hatch, Schmidt would have unhooked his leg and completed the job that he had only half done.

Yet there could be no doubt that he was no longer hostile. One might have supposed he had repented, if it had not been impossible to imagine such a man being given to so weak a feeling as repentance. It was more likely that, having made Landon squeal, he felt that his peculiar brand of honour was satisfied, and that he was now prepared to allow the whole affair to blow away with the warm breezes of the Atlantic Ocean. Landon realized that there was no way of fathoming the mentality that lay behind the scarred cheeks, the pale pig-eyes, and the sun-scorched forehead of this man who had once wielded the whip for Roehm. Perhaps his change of heart was genuine; perhaps he had convinced himself that he really had saved Landon from death, and loved him for that reason, as men will always love the person they have saved. It was impossible to tell what was passing in his mind; but it was advisable to be wary.

"He's still a swine," Green said. "You don't want to run away with the idea that there's been some magic change in his character. That sort of thing don't happen — not in real life, not with men like Schmidt."

Of Golbek Landon saw very little. His work did not bring him much into contact with the steward, and only when he went to collect rations or cigarettes did he approach him closely. Then the eyes were as dead and cold as ever, the face expressionless. There was no reading Golbek's thoughts either, no way of divining whether he meant to do his killing now or this night, or whether he had decided to wait. Golbek gave nothing away; he seemed to have no passions, no feelings. If questioned, he answered briefly in his soft, lisping woman's voice; his small white hands remained motionless, not aiding speech in the Latin way.

Apparently he did not smoke cigarettes, for there were no nicotine stains on his fingers or lips, and a pipe would have seemed ludicrous in his mouth.

But there was always hanging about him that odour of cheap scent that Landon found as repellent as the man himself. Again and again he was angry with himself for allowing such a mean and despicable creature to disturb his peace of mind. But he knew that his was no idle fear; a man like Golbek with a gun or a knife in his hand was as dangerous as a gorilla like Schmidt, with muscles of iron — more dangerous, in fact, by reason of his lack of emotion and the almost clinical detachment that he brought to the business of killing.

"He puts me in mind of a slug," Landon told Green. "A slug leaving a slimy trail wherever it goes."

"You wouldn't be worrying about a slug," Green said. "A thing like that couldn't do you any harm."

Landon agreed. "I was simply thinking about the impression he makes on you. I'd like to know just what he's waiting for. Hell and damnation! I wish he'd make a move — do something."

"And you are that keen to be bumped off? If I was you I'd be glad he was keeping quiet."

I know, I know. That's all very well. But you see how it is: if he started something then I might finish it and get the whole thing settled, one way or the other."

"You mean wipe him out?"

"That's about it. But as it is, I can't do a thing. And all the time he's there — waiting."

"It's the devil right enough," Green said.

The ship sailed north-eastward, across the equator, across the great stream of fresh water flowing into the ocean from the mouth of the Amazon, round the northern corner of Trinidad, and into the warm waters of the Caribbean Sea.

It was for the Gulf of Venezuela that she was bound, there to take on the liquid gold of the Venezuelan oil-fields, the liquid gold that had built great cities like Caracas and had bought the cars and swimming-pools of the millionaires, the fine clothes and jewels of their wives and mistresses.

They came to their destination early, with the haze of morning still upon the land and the sun not risen in all its burning power. The pipes were connected and the cargo began to flow into the tanks of the ship.

"Oil," Green said — "black, dirty, slimy, stinking oil; and it can give you anything in the world. You sink a shaft into the desert, up comes a spout of filthy muck that you can't eat and you can't drink, and there you are, as rich as Solomon in all his glory. Oil that makes the wheels of the world go round: here it is — gallons of it, tons of it, thousands of tons going into this ship, enough to make you or me rich for life; and what do we get for our labour? Chicken-feed. There's uneven distribution of wealth for you."

"Are you a Communist?" Landon asked.

"Only when I'm broke. Give me a thousand quid and you wouldn't catch me yelling for share and share alike."

The black oil, the liquid gold, poured into the tanks of the *Gloria del Mar*, forcing her down into the water, lower and lower at her moorings. The stench of oil hung over the ship like a soiled blanket. At night the shore lights glittered, reflected in the water.

"We can go ashore," Green said. "You coming? Lovely girls, music, dancing, bright lights, everything — maybe. What you say?"

"You take the liberty boat," Landon said. "I'm staying on board."

"You might not get another chance. It don't take long to load this stuff. We'll be away pretty soon."

"It can't be too soon for me."

He was not keen to go ashore. The ship was his link with Philadelphia and New York. He felt that to leave it would be to court bad luck. Ashore, who knew what might happen? He might never get back. True, there was no safety on board, for Golbek was there; but if he went ashore Golbek might follow, and he had had enough of being followed in Buenos Aires. On board ship the area to guard was at least restricted. Besides which, he had no desire for the pleasures of a trip ashore; he had one desire only; and that was to reach New York and Mr Delgado with the least possible delay.

"You go. I'm staying on board."

Green shrugged his shoulders. "Please yourself. But we could have had a time together, you and me. Maybe I'll take Paddy; but it won't be the same."

With Green ashore, Landon felt deserted. He had not realised until then how much the presence of his cabin-mate had meant to him. Green could not give him physical protection, but there was encouragement in the mere fact that he was there — a friend. Now that he was ashore Landon had no friend at all in the ship. He was alone.

Sitting in his cabin, smoking a cigarette, he allowed his mind to dwell upon that loneliness. If he were to die, if Golbek should succeed in killing him, who would mourn his death? Who would miss him? Green perhaps, for a day or two. Gloria Swindon? How long would he stay in her mind if he failed to turn up in New York? Not long. And who else was there to whom his death would mean anything but a brief nuisance? A few relations in England whom he had been in the habit of visiting seldom, of corresponding with never; they would not mourn his passing. He was solitary — a man without ties, without roots. Well, it had always been so, and it had not

238

worried him. Why then should he begin to let it trouble him now? Perhaps he was getting old. At forty-one? To hell with that thought. There was plenty of life in him yet — as Golbek might find to his cost.

Impatiently he stubbed out the half-smoked cigarette and went out on deck, where the 'No Smoking' signs were up. Clusters of lamps showed up the black, flexible pipes that carried the oil into the ship. It was a warm night, and there was no sufficient breeze even to stir the loosely hanging lamps. The ship did not move; the shadows were stationary.

Landon rested his forearms on the rail at the end of the cat-walk and looked towards the bridge. He saw a man in a white jacket standing motionless by the starboard rails and knew that it was Golbek. He too was staying on board. Landon saw his head move round as he gazed aft. He seemed to nod slightly, as though in recognition, though he was too far away and too much in the shadow of the superstructure for his face to be visible. Probably it wore no expression; probably it was as dead and unfeeling as ever. Then he turned away, one shoulder drooping below the other, and went into the accommodation with his shuffling, dragging step.

Landon slept alone in his cabin. Green and McNulty did not come aboard until the morning, and they looked very much the worse for wear.

"You should have come," Green said. "We had a time of it."

Landon looked at him keenly, amusement twitching the corners of his thin, straight mouth. "I believe you. And now you look like death warmed up on a sulky fire."

Green made an effort to straighten his drooping shoulders. The movement seemed to send a spasm of pain shooting up into his head. He winced, but answered with some attempt at dignity: "What you mean — death warmed up? I'm as fit as a fiddle. Just a bit of a thirst — that's all."

"I suppose you want a hair of the dog."

"Not me. I never did believe in that cure. Just plain, clear, fresh, cold water — gallons of it."

He slumped on to the settee in the cabin, looking up at Landon with red-rimmed eyes, his black hair like a tangled mass of seaweed. "You had a quiet time of it? No larks from our dear friend amidships?"

"None at all." Landon did not tell Green that he had slept with the door locked and the porthole clamped shut. The cabin had been over-hot, but he had felt safer.

Green said: "He's not likely to start anything while we're here. It'd be easier and safer at sea. I think you can sleep quiet until we sail."

They heard the bosun's thick, rasping voice: "Come along, then. Plenty of vork to do. Damn all you sore heads. You got to vork, vork, vork."

"Hell with him!" Green said. "Don't he have normal feelings? He was drunk as the best last night, and here he is in the morning as bright as ever. Don't he feel nothing in that head of his? Is it made of iron?"

"I shouldn't wonder," Landon said. "I shouldn't wonder in the least."

* * *

The *Gloria del Mar*, clear of the channel, came to a stop ready to drop the pilot. She was low in the water now, with the dead weight of the oil pulling her down. She had the rich produce of Venezuela in her tanks, a fortune in one ship. But the oil was not hers; she was only the carrier, the means by which it passed from the wells of Venezuela to the refineries of the United States. For this carrying she earned but a fraction of the value of the cargo; but it was enough — it had made the Greek shipowner a millionaire many times over. He never touched the black liquid himself, never even saw it; but it had bought him a private yacht, properties in France and Spain and California, a collection of artistic treasures, and a voice in the secret councils of the world.

But Landon, using the ship as a means to an end, had never seen the owner — did not even know his name. For all his millions, the Greek had less influence on the life of Harvey Landon than a man worth but a fraction of his wealth

— Hermann Schmidt, the bosun.

The pilot-boat came scudding towards the ship, the flag of Venezuela fluttering at its stern and a white curl of foam at its bows. It passed under the *Gloria del Mar's* counter, its engine *put-putting* fussily, and round to the starboard side, down which a Jacob's ladder was dangling.

Landon heard a sudden yell from the bosun: "Hey, you! Come here. Help the passenger aboard."

Landon ran towards him, not giving him any cause for complaint. He was still being wary of the bosun.

"Passenger?"

Schmidt growled: "That's vot I say. You never heard of passengers, maybe?"

"Yes, but I thought — "

"Never mind vot you think. You do vot I tell, pronto."

Landon knew the *Gloria del Mar* had accommodation for five or six passengers, but there had been none on board for the voyage from Buenos Aires, and this seemed to be a very belated boarding. It was not the usual thing for passengers to come out in the pilot-boat; it was leaving things till the last minute with a vengeance. However, it was none of his business. He moved to the Jacob's ladder and looked over the rails at the launch, now close alongside.

The pilot, a short, stout Venezuelan, was coming down from the bridge, saying good-bye to Captain Sharpe; but already the passenger had started to climb the Jacob's ladder. It was a man, and he was dressed in a pearl-grey linen suit, with a wide-brimmed hat on his head. He climbed the ladder rather clumsily, like one not used to such things — not as a sailor would have climbed.

Landon saw a thick wrist covered with black hairs; he saw a watch on the wrist. He knew that watch. It was his own. The head of the passenger came up over the rails; he was sweating a little from the exertion of the climb. He pushed the hat back from his forehead, and Landon saw the white line of the scar ringing it, disappearing behind the ears.

The man looked at him and smiled, his white teeth flashing. It was Captain Garcia, of the Central Republican police.

# 14

## Bound for Philadelphia

"THEY don't seem to trust our Mister Golbek," Green said. "They mean to keep an eye on him — see he does his work properly. Where did you say you left this character, Garcia?"

"The last I saw of him was in a hotel in Almagro just over the border from Argentina."

"You couldn't be mistaken, could you? I happen to have heard that this man is a Bolivian — name of Torres — going to the States on business."

"That may be what his passport says; but I know him. You've seen the scar round his forehead? Not likely there's two like that. Besides, he's wearing my wristwatch. He took it from me in Santa Ana."

"You can't nicely claim it back now, can you? It'd take some explaining."

245

"I may get it just the same."

"You better mind your step. Lucky you've made peace with Schmidt, else you might have had three jokers to deal with. You've got enough on your plate as it is. How do you rate your chances of getting to New York now?"

"I'll manage."

"Maybe you will; maybe you won't." Green pushed his hands into the pockets of his dungaree trousers, turned his back on Landon, and stared out of the porthole. Three miles away, across the rippling, dark-blue waters of the Caribbean sea, another ship was visible, travelling in the same direction as the *Gloria del Mar*, a plume of smoke, like a smudged pencil-mark on the sky, trailing from her funnel. Between the two ships a flight of birds swooped down, hovered above the water, then soared like a tattered kite into the sky.

"Know what I'd do if I was in your shoes?" Green said.

"What?"

"I'd go along to Torres or Garcia, or whatever his name is, and I'd strike a bargain. I'd say to him, 'Look, you can

246

have the letter for a thousand dollars, on condition you call off your bloodhound.' It'd save a whole lot of unpleasantness all round."

"No," Landon said.

"No? Well, it's your skin, not mine; but speaking for myself, I'd be only too willing to give up four thousand dollars for the chance of living a bit longer, horrible as this old world most certainly is. In fact, I don't know that I wouldn't give up the whole lot."

He turned away from the porthole, slid his long, thin body on to the settee, and stared up at Landon. "That's my opinion, for what it's worth."

"You don't understand," Landon said. "It isn't simply a question of dollars. Don Diego is my friend. I've given him my word that I'll deliver the letter — or, if that's not possible, that I won't let it fall into the hands of Romero's bastards. This is something that has nothing to do with dollars — "

He broke off, his face reddening. Stated like this, it all sounded so damned heroic — all honour and that sort of stuff, that Green probably thought him a fool to worry about. Well then, he was a fool; he accepted the fact. But he would go on being a fool. Whatever happened, he would make no bargain with Garcia even if the chance were offered to him. He knew that if the positions had been reversed Don Diego would have died rather than betray him. Could he rate his own honour at a lower value than that of his friend?

Green was looking at him slyly, one eyebrow lifted. "So that's the way of it," he said. "I didn't realize. I thought you were just a soldier of fortune, open to anybody's bid." He sucked in his breath sharply. "Well, pal, I hope you make it."

★ ★ ★

The days passed; the ship drove northward, threading her way between the islands. Now and again a sudden squall would blow up from nowhere, ruffling the surface of the sea and patching it with white, as if a painter had swept his brush across it, touching only the crests of the waves. Rain would fall in brief, violent showers, cooling the iron of the decks and bringing out the sharp, sweet odour of damp timbers. Then the squall would pass as quickly as it had appeared, the clouds would slide away from the face of the sun, and in a moment the decks would be steaming under the heat.

And Garcia bided his time. Landon saw him only occasionally — sunning himself on deck, smoking a cigar, sitting in the shade of an awning; he appeared to be nothing but what he gave himself out to be: a businessman taking a passage to Philadelphia. But once, when Landon was on his way to the wheelhouse, Garcia had appeared suddenly from a doorway, smiled, and said: "Good morning, Señor Landon. I hope you are enjoying good health — so far."

Landon had gone by without a word, but he had heard Garcia's throaty chuckle following him, mocking him with his inability to escape.

He wondered why Garcia had been sent rather than another man. Perhaps it was because Garcia knew him. Or perhaps this was a chance for the policeman to redeem his failure in allowing a prisoner to escape. Whatever the reason, it was certain that Garcia would be doubly keen not to make a second mistake.

And still he made no moves.

"It's a war of nerves, that's what it is," Green said. "He's trying to get you on edge. He's playing with you like a cat with a mouse. Only I wouldn't say as you was exactly a mouse."

It was a few hundred miles north of the Bahamas that the gale struck the ship. It was no hurricane, but it turned the main deck of the *Gloria del Mar* into a foaming torrent, so that it was possible to move fore and aft only along the cat-walks. The cat-walks were like narrow bridges thrown across boiling mountain rivers, and as the ship rolled, boring her way through the seas, the wind sent sheets of spray flying over her upperworks, leaving the white rime of salt on everything, the taste of salt in the very air.

"A bit of a blow," Green said. "It won't last long."

"How do you know?" Landon asked.

"I've seen these storms before. They

soon blow themselves out. This one will too."

Landon thought Green might be right, though he might just as easily be wrong. Green considered himself something of a weather-prophet, more reliable than any barometer; but the results did not always support his faith in himself. Landon remembered an evening when he had looked at the sky and had predicted half a gale before morning. In the event it had been a dead calm night, but Green had brazened it out. "The Old Man must have altered course to avoid it. The weather was there all right."

Landon hoped the gale would pass quickly. The rolling of the ship did not affect his stomach, for that was inured to sea-sickness. But the discomfort of having meals sliding off the mess table, cups spilling their contents in your face when you tried to drink, of being tumbled from side to side in your bunk as you attempted to sleep, of being drenched from head to foot with sea-water when you went on watch — all these were experiences that in his younger days he had accepted with a certain sense of adventure, but which, now that he was older, he looked upon simply as a damned nuisance.

Now, he thought, was surely the opportunity for Garcia and Golbek to do their job. At night they need only wait for him to go for his spell in the wheelhouse, shoot him down or drive a silent knife into his back, and throw his body overboard. In this howling gale no one would be likely to hear a pistol shot; in the blackness of the storm-ravaged night no one would see him go. And the explanation of his disappearance would be so easy: he had been washed overboard by one of the heavy seas that were continually raking the ship. It could all be so simple. And, realizing the simplicity of it, Landon took extra care, moving swiftly past the dark places of the ship, treading cat-like across the swilling decks.

The next morning he could have laughed at his fears and precautions. Then he saw Golbek hanging on to the starboard rails as though his hands had been welded there. He was bent at the waist, as though some one had gripped the two halves of his body and had begun to fold one upon the other; his head was hanging over the side, and he seemed to be looking down at the waves that ran lashing and foaming past, as if debating whether to fling himself into them and finish his agony once and for all. His face was green, and his hair, blown about by the wind, a salty tangle; every other minute he retched painfully, but he seemed long since to have emptied his stomach, for nothing came up. Landon gazed at him for a while, then went on. If Garcia was in a similar condition he need have no fear of either man until the storm had passed.

For once Green's weather forecast was correct. The gale died quickly, the seas calmed, and the ship forged northward into the colder latitudes off the American coast. Landon was glad of the thicker clothing that he had bought in Buenos Aires. The cabin and the mess-room became more attractive refuges from the bitter exposure of the open deck. He had been so long in the warmth of the southern summer and the heat of the tropics that he felt this cold keenly. But he knew that there would be worse to follow when they had pressed even farther north. It was still January — mid-winter in the northern hemisphere. There would be snow and ice to come, no doubt about that.

It was midnight on the day following the storm when he saw Garcia again. He was coming down the ladder from the navigating bridge when Garcia, huddled in a thick overcoat, stepped forward then put a hand on his arm as he reached the bottom.

"Señor Landon," he said. "I would like to speak to you."

Landon stood still. So things were moving at last. Garcia was about to show his hand; the bluffing was finished. He peered into the shadows, searching for the shape of Golbek; but he could not see him.

"And if I do not wish to talk to you?" he said.

He wondered what exactly Garcia's purpose was. They would not kill him here; that was certain. It was too near the bridge; there were men up there, only a few yards away. What then did Garcia hope to do? Lure him into a dark corner where he or Golbek could use a knife? Somehow he did not think that Garcia would do his own killing — not with Golbek to call upon.

"Do not make things awkward," Garcia said softly. "It is for your own good, I assure you. You wish to save your skin?"

"I have no intention of dying," Landon said. He could hear the officer of the watch striding back and forth along the starboard wing of the bridge, a man coughing, the gentle clacking of some loose tackle, the hiss of water being thrust aside by the ship: all these sounds, coming out of the darkness, seemed so normal that it was unimaginable that the man beside him should be speaking coldly and calmly of murder. Yet he knew that the softness of Garcia's voice was deceptive, that the purpose behind it was iron-hard, impervious to pleading or feelings of pity.

"Your intentions are not important," Garcia said. "I am interested only in my own convenience. I think we can come to an agreement that will be to our mutual advantage. Come; what harm can there be in talking matters over like civilized beings? Let us go to my cabin, have a drink, a cigar perhaps, a talk. What do you say?"

Landon hesitated. Should he agree to Garcia's suggestion? He did not know what purpose lay behind it, though he felt sure that it was nothing for his good. But he was sick of uncertainty, of not knowing when or where his enemy would strike. If he talked with Garcia he might at least be able to peer into the man's mind, to glean some inkling of his intentions. True, it might be a trap; but what need had they to trap him? He was there always. They knew he could not escape; he would have needed to be a powerful swimmer to do that. Besides, he did not think that Garcia would attempt to kill him in the cabin. It was too close to the officers' quarters; a pistol shot would be heard; a knife would be messy. No; it was out on the open deck that they would try to kill him when the time came — in the darkness, with the sea to swallow up his dead body.

"I will come," he said at last. "But you go first. I'll follow."

Garcia chuckled. "You think perhaps I try to strike you in the back? No, no; I would not do a thing like that. You can trust me."

"I'd sooner trust a rattlesnake," Landon said.

He sensed rather than saw the shrug of Garcia's shoulders. "As you wish. You see I trust you, though perhaps I have good reason not to do so."

He turned and moved away from the bridge ladder, Landon following close behind him. If this was a trick to bring him within range of Golbek's gun, Garcia would be in almost as must danger as he. But his fears were groundless. They saw no one on the way to Garcia's cabin, and in less than a minute they were inside.

"You see," Garcia said. "You suspected me without cause. Really, if you only knew it, I am the best friend you possess at the present moment. Certainly I am the only one who can help you in a very unpleasant situation — yes, very unpleasant."

He took off his thick coat and hung it

on a peg at the back of the door. The cabin was fairly large, as such cabins go; it contained a double bed, a wardrobe, a wash-basin in a recess, a table, and two armchairs. Garcia indicated one of the chairs with a flutter of his hand.

"Please sit down. It is much less tiring to talk while sitting." He went to the recess, ferreted in a cupboard under the wash-basin, and came up with a bottle of whisky and two glasses. He put the glasses on the table and filled them. He handed one to Landon.

"But you are still standing. It is not necessary. I assure you nothing is going to happen to you. Do sit down."

Landon took the drink, pulled a chair close to the bulk-head on one side of the cabin, and sat down, his oilskin coat crackling under him.

"That is better," Garcia said. "Now we can talk. You will have a cigar?"

"No, thank you."

"No? But you do not mind if I do?"

"Get down to business," Landon said harshly. "I've been on watch. I want some sleep."

"Ah, of course." Garcia took a cigar

for himself, cut it and lit it with leisurely precision, an expression of concentration on his dark, heavy face. "You wish to sleep. But not, I think, the big sleep that lasts until the Day of Judgment. You do not wish for that sleep, eh, Señor Landon?"

Landon drank some of the whisky. It was genuine Scotch. His opinion of Garcia's taste rose slightly. But he wished the fellow would not beat about the bush so much.

"Come to the point," he said.

Garcia leaned back in his chair, holding the cigar between two plump fingers, Landon's watch still strapped to his heavy wrist.

"The point," he said, "is that you do not wish to die and I do not wish to kill you."

"No?"

"No. Believe me, I speak the truth. It seems to me so unnecessary, so useless."

"And Golbek?"

"Ah, Golbek! Now there is a man of quite a different mentality, a man who enjoys killing for its own sake. I should like to tell you something about that man." Garcia lost his air of languid unconcern and leaned forward, gripping the arms of the chair. "He is, as perhaps you already know, a Pole. But not a patriot — far from it. He was in Poland in 1939 when the Germans moved in; but he did not fight the Germans — he was too clever for that — he worked for them. They were very grateful to Golbek; they paid him well for betraying his own people, putting the finger on resistance fighters and trouble-makers of that sort. The Germans even employed him to do some of their killing, and he enjoyed that. You have guessed that he is not entirely as other men — subnormal, shall we say? Possibly it is that subnormality that has produced in him a hatred of his fellow creatures, giving him his particular pleasure in killing. An interesting psychological point, that. Don't you agree?"

"Go on," Landon said. He was fascinated by Garcia's black, velvety eyes. They were fixed on him as Garcia talked, watching his reactions.

"I doubt whether Golbek himself knows how many men he has murdered.

He is completely without compunction or remorse; it is doubtful whether he has any conception of the meaning of the words. I should think the Nazi occupation of Poland was the happiest time of his life, but, unfortunately for him, it did not last; the German army withdrew, and there was our poor friend Golbek left high and dry. But Golbek was clever. He did not wait for the Russians or the Polish patriots to take revenge upon him; he slipped across the border, made his way to Rostock, and somehow got across to Sweden. For some reason or other he was not well liked there, and before long he had popped up in Mexico, that refuge of all political martyrs. Since then he has worked in Nicaragua, Cuba, Bolivia, Argentina, and many other places."

"Worked?"

"At his trade — killing. I tell you all this, Señor Landon, so that you may have no illusions regarding the kind of man with whom you have to deal. It must have been very difficult indeed for him to curb his natural instincts — under our orders — from the time this ship left Buenos Aires to the present moment."

"Under your orders?"

Garcia smiled. "But of course. You do not suppose he has failed to kill you because he could not? That would be to mislead yourself. Left to his own devices he would have finished the job long ago. And, of course, he has added reason to kill you because you made a fool of him. His professional pride was injured, and there is only one way in which it can be restored. Besides which, you hurt him physically by a blow on the jaw."

"I wish it had been a permanent injury," Landon said. "How did he trace me to the ship?"

Garcia leaned back again and puffed at his cigar. "Ah, there he was clever. You will remember that you left him lying in a warehouse, and that you ran out and caught a taxi?"

"Yes."

"Well, Golbek recovered almost at once; he was in time to catch the number of the taxi. It was not until next day that he was able to trace it; and that was after he had paid a visit to your lodging-house and found that you had

262

flown. From the taxi-driver he learned where you had spent the previous night. He made further inquiries; he found a girl. You must have been very drunk that night. You told her such a lot; and I am sure a careful man like you would not have done so if you had been sober. It was fortunate for us, of course."

Landon's jaw tightened. So it had been the girl who had given him away. And yet he could not blame her. It was he himself who had been to blame. He had drunk too much and had talked.

"I see," he said.

"You do see, don't you? You see what I mean about Golbek being keen to kill you. But I am not. Señor Landon, I do not dislike you. You may not believe me, but I am a man of peace." He lifted one of his hands, as if to prevent any expression of disagreement. "Ah, I know what you would say: how can a policeman be a man of peace? But it is so. I love law and order; I detest violence. Violence is sometimes necessary, but I deplore its use. It is so — shall we say — barbaric."

He was smiling now. One might have supposed that he was indeed a man full of benevolence, of love for his fellow creatures. That they had not always treated him kindly was proved by the white scar circling his forehead; but the smile was there to persuade one that he was of a forgiving nature, that he could even overlook a gaol-break that had without debut been a blow to his prestige.

Landon was not persuaded. He knew that Garcia wanted something, that he had a proposal to make and was taking the devil of a time to make it.

"Come to the point," he said again.

"You have a letter," Garcia said. "You are to be paid five thousand dollars for delivering it to a Señor Delgado in New York. You see I have my facts."

"Well?"

"I should like that letter. It is all I want from you. Not your life. Do you not think it would be sensible for you to sell it to me?"

"Alvear made that proposal. The answer is still the same — no."

"Alvear. Why, yes, but then you did

264

not know that your life was in danger. You knew nothing of Golbek. I ask you not to be stupid. Whatever happens, you will not be allowed to deliver the letter. Why not, therefore, take one thousand dollars and your life rather than make unpleasantness? After all, you do not know that Delgado will pay the five thousand even if you should manage to contact him."

"When would you pay your money?"

"In Philadelphia. I could not get the dollars until then."

"And are you prepared to wait for the letter until we reach Philadelphia?"

"Oh, no," Garcia said. "You cannot expect me to do that. I must have the letter now. But you will be paid, never fear. You have it on you?"

Landon did not move. He was not such a fool as to believe what Garcia had said. The only grain of truth in it was the fact that Garcia wanted the letter. The thousand dollars promise was moonshine; the protestation that he disliked killing was moonshine also. If Landon handed over the letter he would be no safer than before. Garcia could not allow him to go free even then, for, as far as Garcia knew, he might be carrying a verbal message also that could be as harmful to the Romero cause as the written one. No; Golbek still had his work to do.

Landon stood up, the oilskin rustling. He put his empty whisky glass on the table.

"We're wasting time," he said. "I need some sleep. Thanks for the drink."

The smile left Garcia's face. He saw that he had been throwing away his eloquence, that this man was not as gullible as he had taken him to be. When he spoke his voice had lost its soft, caressing quality; it was harsh — the voice of Captain Garcia, the policeman, accustomed to the giving of orders.

"You will not leave this cabin."

"Don't try to stop me," Landon said. He began to move towards the door — warily, watching Garcia's hands, watching for a gun.

Garcia did not move from his chair. He simply raised his voice a little and spoke one word: "Golbek!"

The door behind Landon opened

quietly, and Golbek slipped into the cabin. He shut the door behind him, locked it, and dropped the key into his pocket. Then he stood with his back to the door and waited.

# 15

## Persuasion

FOR the space of a quarter of a minute there was silence in the cabin, broken only by the sound of Golbek's hastened breathing and the creaking of the wardrobe door. The ship was rolling slightly, just enough to make it necessary to counteract with a scarcely conscious movement of the body the tilting of the cabin floor, yet not enough to upset the whisky bottle and the glasses standing on the table. But for this movement, it might have been difficult for a person suddenly awaking in the cabin to tell that he was on board a ship, for the porthole was concealed by a print curtain, and the bed, apart from the fact that it was a fixture, had nothing particularly nautical about it. This might, in fact, have been a bed-sitting room in a great city, with acres of concrete and brick surrounding it instead of miles of ocean.

"Sit down," Garcia said at last.

Landon moved back against the bulkhead on the right of the door, but he remained standing.

"You were going to your quarters," Garcia said smoothly; "but now you will have to stay with us for a while longer." He had recovered all his composure; his voice was again soft and oily. It was as though he knew that he was in command of the situation and could afford to take his time.

Golbek had said nothing. He was in his steward's livery, but even a blue serge jacket with silver buttons and a high neck-band could not put any real smartness into his appearance. His left shoulder still drooped below the right, and he still had that strangely shrunken look, so that the jacket did not so much fit him as lodge upon the more prominent parts of his body. At the chest it seemed to fold inward, as though there were nothing beneath but a hollow space. He stood with his back to the door, his pale, cold eyes moving slowly from Landon to Garcia and back again to

Landon. The odour of cheap scent hung about him like an invisible cloak.

"You do not wish to sit?" Garcia said. "Very well. For myself, I never stand when I can make use of a chair. The saving of energy is not to be ignored. It is my considered opinion that — "

"Get on with it," Landon said. "Don't waste so much time on talking."

Garcia puffed out his dark cheeks. He had not shaved since morning, and the stiff bristles were clearly visible around his mouth and in the folds of his chin.

"You are impatient. You should not be. No man should be impatient for ill treatment."

"Ill treatment?"

"If you refuse to agree to my most reasonable proposals it will unfortunately be necessary to use — persuasion. You do not deny that you have the letter on you?"

Once again Landon saw that he had made a mistake. He ought not to have carried the letter with him; he ought to have hidden it in some place other than his cabin, where Golbek and Garcia would not have thought of looking for it.

On board the ship there were hundreds of such hiding-places. But it was too late now — too late even to deny that he had the letter in his pocket. They would not believe him.

"As I thought," Garcia said. "Golbek assures me that he made a thorough search of your quarters before I joined the ship. He is experienced in such activities; I did not think he would have overlooked the letter if it had been there. Come now, are you ready to hand it over and save trouble?"

"Trouble for you or for me?"

Garcia smiled. He laid his cigar in an ash-tray on the table and rubbed his hands together. "Señor Landon, the odds are two to one. Figure for yourself who is likely to be hurt. Be sensible."

Landon jerked a thumb at Golbek. "Tell this filth to unlock the door."

Garcia made an almost imperceptible movement of his hand, and Golbek sprang at Landon. He seemed to bunch himself suddenly into a ball and project himself through the air. Landon had been expecting a move, but this came with so little warning that before he could take any action on his own part Golbek's hands were clawing at his throat, and Golbek's stinking breath was fanning his face.

But he knew how to break that hold. He brought his own hands up and struck sharply and viciously upward at Golbek's elbows. Golbek gave a yelp like a puppy that some one had stamped on, and the grip on Landon's throat loosened. Landon thrust forward with both hands, and Golbek's body thudded against the bulkhead on the opposite side of the cabin.

Then both of them were on him, forcing him to the floor. He felt a cord circling his neck. It tightened, cutting into his throat. He brought his knees up violently into Garcia's belly; Garcia grunted, but held on. Landon's body was like a steel spring, coiling and uncoiling, but he could not free his neck from the tightening cord.

He could not breathe; it was like a knife cutting across his windpipe; the blood roared in his ears. He summoned up all his strength for a last heave, and found that his legs were clamped to the floor by the dead weight of Garcia's body. The roaring in his ears increased; a black and red curtain seemed to sway in front of his eyes. He felt himself falling into a pit, whirling round and round . . .

Then, suddenly, the pressure on his throat relaxed. The air came bubbling, sucking into his lungs. The curtain moved away from his eyes.

Garcia and Golbek were still holding him down, but they were motionless; they seemed to be listening. The drumming in Landon's ears subsided gradually, and he listened too, wondering what it was that had disturbed the other two — had saved him from strangulation. Then he heard it also — the sound of footsteps in the alley-way outside the cabin, staggering footsteps that seemed to go past and then return, as though the man outside could not make up his mind where he wanted to go.

Landon opened his mouth to yell, and Golbek thrust a filthy handkerchief into it, shutting off the cry. The handkerchief reeked of Golbek's peculiar brand of scent; it made Landon retch.

The footsteps finally came to a halt just outside the door, and they could hear a mumbling voice, like that of a man talking to himself, carrying on a single-handed argument. Then, so suddenly that each of the three inside the cabin started with the shock, he began to sing in a wailing, high-pitched voice:

"Oh, whishky ish the life of man. Whishky Johnnie . . . "

After a few lines he stopped singing and twisted the knob of the cabin door, swearing to himself as he did so. Since the door would not open he began to kick it, grumbling at the same time: "Who's lock bloody door? No right lock doors. Open, you bashtards. Open thish door, blasht you!"

Neither Garcia nor Golbek moved, and the kicking became furious. Then, as suddenly as it started, it ceased, and they heard a chuckle, full of self-satisfaction, like that of a man delighted with his own cleverness. After that there was silence for perhaps half a minute, while the three in the cabin waited, the tension growing with every second that passed.

Landon's hopes sank. He supposed

that the man must have gone away after failing to get into the cabin. He wanted to call out, but the handkerchief stuffed in his mouth and held there by Golbek's hand prevented him from doing so. He felt sick. He had always been nauseated by Golbek's scent; now he had it in his mouth, the detested odour catching at his throat.

He had not heard the man's footsteps going away, but he supposed the fellow must have gone; he would surely not have been standing outside the door all this while. In another moment Garcia would think so too, and the cord would tighten again.

He heard Garcia sigh, a long forcing-out of pent-up breath. The grip on the cord tightened.

But this time there was a different, even more startling interruption. Four pistol shots fired in rapid succession ripped away the lock of the door, a heavy kick crashed it open, and there stood Captain Sharpe, with a revolver in his right hand.

"Keep me out, would ye? No man keeps old Sharpe out of any cabin board hish own ship. No man."

Garcia whipped the cord away from Landon's neck and stuffed it into his pocket. He got up from the floor, jerking Golbek to his feet also. Landon, finding himself suddenly free, pulled the handkerchief from his mouth and stood up too. One look at Sharpe was enough to tell him that the captain was drunk, even if his slurred speech and his irresponsible actions had not already made that fact plain. He teetered backward and forward, apparently hardly able to stand on his feet; the revolver swaying dangerously.

"Who are ye, anyway? I don't know ye — any of ye. Where d'ye come from?" His head was thrust forward, vulture-like. He peered at them with his beady, bloodshot eyes, trying to get things into focus. "Damn foreigners! Bashtards — the whole stinking lot of ye. Not fit to shcrub decks. Sh — sh — shcum, filth, rats' dung! T'hell wi' the whole caboodle. T'hell!"

The revolver exploded in his hand, Golbek leaped to one side, and the bullet splintered the glass in the wardrobe door. Captain Sharpe fell on his face and lay where he had fallen.

At that moment the mate and the chief steward appeared in the alley-way, with dressing-gowns over their pyjamas.

"What's going on here?" the mate asked. "Who was shooting?"

Landon stepped forward. "It was Captain Sharpe. He's blind drunk. We'd better get him to his own cabin."

He picked up the revolver and handed it to the mate. Then with the help of the chief steward he lifted Sharpe from the floor and carried him into the alley-way. Sharpe made neither protest nor resistance; he was fast asleep. Garcia and Golbek stood on one side, watching Landon go and saying not a word.

Landon left Captain Sharpe in the care of the mate and chief steward, and went to his own cabin. Across the cat-walk he ran quickly, bent low, making as small a target of himself as possible. But there was no shot, no sign whatever of Garcia or Golbek. For the moment it seemed that they had accepted defeat.

Landon went into his cabin, but did not switch on the light, not wishing to wake Green, who was asleep in the upper bunk. He took off his oilskin coat and felt inside his jacket for the letter in its oilcloth wrapper. He found it, went out of the cabin again, and climbed to the deck above, where the lifeboats were. Feeling his way in the darkness to the port boat, he began to loosen the canvas cover stretched over it. When enough of the cover was loose he slipped it back and climbed into the boat. After groping about for a short while he found what he was searching for — a box of stores wrapped round with canvas, to keep the water out. He untied the wrapping, slipped the letter underneath, and tied it up again. Then he climbed out of the lifeboat and refastened the cover.

At least the letter was now safe from Garcia. He would never find it in such a hiding-place. Landon felt some grain of satisfaction. Even if they killed him, Romero's sharks would gain no information.

The following morning he had a brief interview with Captain Sharpe — at his own request. Sharpe, sitting at a table in his own cabin, was not in a good temper. He looked sick and even more shrivelled than usual, his neck sticking up through the collar of his shirt like the fleshless, stringy invention of some ultra-modern sculptor.

To Landon's complaint that the passenger, Torres, and the steward, Golbek, had attacked him and had, in fact, attempted to strangle him, Sharpe turned an unsympathetic ear, answering in his squeaky, unoiled voice: "Bilge! Don't bring damned idiotic tales to me. I'm too busy to listen to the ravings of a bloody lunatic. Why should they wish to kill you?"

"I can't tell you that, sir. I can only tell you the facts."

"Facts! Stuff and nonsense! Hell, man; is this all you wanted to see me about? I thought it was something important. Wasting my time with cock-and-bull stories."

Landon persisted, though he had already guessed the futility of doing so. "But you must see, sir, that I am telling the truth. Last night, if it hadn't been for you, they would have finished the job. You saw them. It was only your intervention that stopped them."

Captain Sharpe's face darkened with anger; it was as though what little blood there was in his dried-up husk of a body had all rushed upward to colour his neck, his cheeks, and his forehead. His voice rose to a higher pitch than ever; it was almost a scream.

"What do you mean, damn you? What do you mean? I saw nothing last night. I don't know what you're blabbering about. You're mad, that's what it is; you're mad. You've been imagining things. I've seen fellows like you before. You want to keep a watch on yourself or you'll be in real trouble. We've got a cell for lunatics, and you may find yourself inside it if you go on in this way. D'you hear me?"

He had worked himself up into a fury with this tirade. He jumped to his feet, beating on the table with his fists, his nose thrust forward like a lance, and his tiny, ferret-eyes glowing. Then suddenly a spasm seemed to pass through him; he gave a little gasp of pain and sat down abruptly, one side of his face twitching uncontrollably. He was panting, gasping for breath. He made a fluttering motion with one skinny, vein-ridged hand.

"Get to hell out of here. Go on. Get out."

Landon looked at the glaring eyes and pain-racked face and wondered whether the captain had had some kind of stroke.

"Are you all right, sir?" he asked. "Is there anything I can do for you?"

Captain Sharpe's anger flamed out again. "Yes, damn you! You can get out."

Landon turned and left the cabin. Glancing back before he shut the door, he saw that Captain Sharpe was resting his elbows on the table, his head cupped in his hands, the grey hair sprouting out above the fingers like the tuft of a very ancient coconut. Landon pulled the door to and walked away. He had been a fool to appeal to the captain, or to hope for any help from that quarter. All he had succeeded in doing was to bring Sharpe's anger on his own head for reminding him of an incident that he obviously wished to forget. With his own sins to answer for, the captain was not likely to root into those of other people.

What could Landon have expected from him? The instant arrest of Garcia and Golbek? The idea was ridiculous. In any case Sharpe had been too drunk to grasp the full meaning of what he had seen in Garcia's cabin. To have taken drastic action against a passenger and a steward on the mere word of a seaman who had come on board in Buenos Aires without papers or recommendation would have been more than anyone could have expected of him, even if he had been sober when he shot the lock off the cabin door. Knowing his own weakness, he would be only too eager to hush the matter up, never to refer to it again. Luckily for him, neither Garcia nor Golbek was likely to make a fuss about the incident.

Landon made his way back to his own quarters across the catwalk, shivering a little in the icy wind coming down from the north. There was snow not far away, and the sea had a grey, cold look, joining itself almost imperceptibly all round the horizon to the grey and threatening sky. The ship was rolling, taking water over the main deck under the cat-walk — water that swilled, foaming white, first to starboard, then to port, like a river unable to decide which way to flow.

Landon saw that there was no hope of getting help from Sharpe. 'Brandy' Sharpe — named with the accuracy and lack of flattery that sailors have — might have been a good captain once, but he had been ruined by the bottle. He was not the first one; he would not be the last. Well, to-morrow the ship would be sailing up the Delaware. If he could keep himself alive for one more night all might be well. He did not imagine that Garcia would abandon his efforts even after the ship was brought alongside in Philadelphia — Garcia himself would have to answer to his superiors for any failure. But once let the ship's side make contact with the firm ground of North America, and Landon believed that he could outwit all his enemies.

# 16

## In the Night

LANDON was shot at as he was moving across the dark parts of the ship between the navigating bridge, where he had been doing his trick at the wheel, and the midships end of the cat-walk. It was just after midnight, and the wind had backed to the north-east, freshening and bringing a curtain of driving snow. It was as Landon had feared earlier in the day; they were running into winter right enough, and the cold was testing the thinness of his blood. He could have used a duffel coat, but he had to make do with a sweater and the oilskin, which was as stiff as a sheet of tin, rustling and crackling as he moved.

He went warily past the midships deckhouse, keeping a sharp look-out. There ought to have been a light, but it was black. Perhaps the bulb had been removed; perhaps it had burnt out. The ship was tossing about a good deal, and the snow on the decks made them slippery and treacherous; in gumboots it was no easy matter to keep a footing. Landon was feeling for the handrail when he heard the crack of the pistol, and a spurt of flame stabbed at him out of the darkness. Almost simultaneously, so that the three sensations of hearing, seeing, and feeling were as one, he felt the flesh of his left forearm burn, as though a red-hot iron had been laid upon it.

It was like a prick goading him, like the starter's gun in a race. Before the gun flamed again he was moving. He heard the bullet clang against some metal obstruction and go whining away into the darkness, joining its lamentation to that of the wind. But he was already slithering towards the ladder at the after end of the deck. He scarcely touched the steps in going down it. At the bottom his feet slid from under him, and he fell heavily. He was up almost at once, his left arm throbbing with fire, and blood dripping down towards his wrist. He had no time to think about his wound; he knew that unless he kept moving there would be nothing for him to think about — ever.

He was blinded by the darkness and the flurrying snow, but he found the cat-walk and began running across it, with the wind buffeting him, the oilskin flapping, and below him the water faintly visible in white streaks of foam, swilling back and forth across the moving deck.

A violent roll of the ship flung him against the cat-walk rails, driving the breath out of him; he grunted with pain. But he could not wait to recover. Golbek would be after him, eager now to finish the job. Would anyone have heard the shots? On such a night of squalling wind and rushing seas it was doubtful. A pistol shot was not so loud that it could not be put down to any one of a great variety of causes, none of which would have merited investigation by a busy officer of the watch. Landon ran on in his clumsy gumboots with the wind at his back, imagining that he heard Golbek's dragging footsteps close upon his heels, expecting at any moment to hear again the pistol crack, to feel a bullet thud into his back.

But he reached the poop safely and

was about to step off the cat-walk when he sensed rather than saw a movement by the rails on his left. He saw the glimmer of a face in the darkness and knew immediately that here was another danger. With hardly a pause he jumped at the shadow and stabbed sharply upward with his knee. He felt the knee sink into a thick belly, heard a man's gasp of pain, and saw his head jerk forward. It was, as he had guessed, Captain Garcia, who had been waiting to cut off his line of retreat.

In Garcia's right hand was a revolver that he had not had the chance to use. He was still gasping in agony when Landon gripped his wrist and banged it hard down on the iron rail. The revolver went spinning away into the darkness.

Landon pulled his knife out of its sheath and dug the point firmly into Garcia's back. He put an arm round Garcia's neck, pulling him on to the knife-point. He could hear Golbek coming, and he spoke fiercely in Garcia's ear.

"Tell him to go away. Not to shoot."

Garcia needed no urging. He was between Golbek and Landon, a target for any marksmanship. He shouted hoarsely: "Stop, Henryk! Don't shoot; don't shoot. It is I, Garcia. Stay where you are."

Landon did not know whether it was that Golbek failed to hear or to understand, or whether it was that the desire to kill drove him on, but he did not obey Garcia's command; he pressed forward, appearing like a ghost out of the snow.

Landon saw his arm come up and knew with absolute certainty that he was going to fire. Garcia realized it too, and with a yell of fear and anger wrenched himself from Landon's grasp and flung himself straight at Golbek, knocking the pistol aside just as Golbek pressed the trigger.

The bullet went singing harmlessly out to sea, and at that moment, the moment when Garcia leaped forward, the ship rolled heavily over to port. The roll added to the momentum of Garcia's rush, and both he and Golbek slipped on the snowy deck and went sliding out of Landon's sight. He heard a wailing cry and then a splash, and, running forward, he found Garcia lying alone by the rails and trying to get to his feet. More cries came from somewhere in the darkness and more sounds of splashing, and Landon guessed that Golbek had slipped down the ladder leading to the flooded main deck. To judge by the cries, the fall had not killed him, but it might well be that he was severely injured. Landon hoped that he was.

At that moment he heard another voice, thick and rasping. "Devil take it! Vot happens out here?"

A broad beam of light shone out from a doorway in the deck-house and in the beam Landon could see the burly, stocky figure of Hermann Schmidt and behind him two or three other members of the crew. They were all fully dressed and had probably been playing cards late into the night.

Schmidt came out into the snow, cursing and grumbling. "Somebody being killed, is it? Somebody overboard? Vot's that blutty yelling?"

Landon slipped quietly away in the darkness and went to his cabin, leaving Garcia to do what explaining he might think fit. Whatever Garcia might tell

Schmidt, he hardly thought it would be the exact truth. He did not think he would have any further trouble from either Golbek or Garcia that night. And to-morrow they would be Philadelphia.

Green woke and sat up in his bunk when Landon switched the light on. He noticed at once the blood dripping from Landon's left hand, and then he saw the hole in the sleeve of the oilskin. He was out of his bunk in one leap.

"Hell! You've hurt yourself."

"Not hurt myself," Landon said. "I've been hurt by some one else. Shot, to be exact. Nothing broken. I can still use the arm."

He was struggling to get the oilskin off. Green helped him. The sleeve of the jacket was soaked in blood from the elbow to the cuff. They got the jacket off and rolled up the sleeve of the shirt, Landon clenching his teeth as the cloth pulled away from the wound. Green looked at it doubtfully.

"You ought to go to the steward with this."

"No; it'll be all right," Landon said. He did not want to make a noise about it.

He wanted no hold-ups in Philadelphia if he could help it. "Get some warm water from the galley. It won't look so bad when it's been washed."

"All right if you think so," Green said, and went away for the water.

Landon was right about the wound. He had been lucky. It was no more than a nick along the surface of the forearm. An adhesive dressing covered it easily.

"Nine inches," Green said.

"Nine inches! What do you mean?"

"The distance between a scratch on the arm and a bullet through the heart. You're the lucky one, and no mistake."

"I just hope the luck holds out," Landon said. "I've been using it pretty fast. I hope I've got some left."

Golbek was lucky too. It was McNulty who brought news of him next morning as the ship was moving into Delware Bay.

"What you think?" McNulty said. "That damn Polak steward was up to some tricks last night — him and Torres, the passenger."

"What happened?" Green asked innocently.

"What happened? Well, I wouldn't be knowing exactly; but they was down this end of the ship. Schmidt thought he heard a gun go off. We said he was dreaming; but then there was a whole lot of yelling, so we went out to look. And what do we find but this Torres sprawled out in the snow and Golbek down there on the main deck, splashing about and screaming fit to but his lungs."

"How did he get down there?"

"Now, how would I know. Maybe Torres pushed him; maybe he just slipped. What can you expect of a damned Polak?"

"Was he hurt much?" Landon asked.

"He was bruised sure enough, but that's about all. He must have dropped feet first. If he'd gone down on his nut he wouldn't have done much yelling, not much more stewarding neither. Wouldn't have been a terrible loss, if you ask me. The puzzle is, what was him and that Torres doing down this end at half-past twelve on a night like last night? Nobody in his senses would have been out at all if he didn't have to be."

"Didn't they say why they were there?"

"Torres mumbled something about losing his way in the dark. There's a tale for you. He must have known when he was on the cat-walk. Golbek wouldn't say a thing; he's a clam if ever there was one. But if you ask me there's something fishy going on between those two — something might not bear looking at too closely."

"There's one thing you can bet on," Green said. "Nobody on board this ship is going to do much looking. They're all too busy keeping their noses in their own business. You better forget it too, Paddy."

"Sure, I'll forget it. I got my own affairs."

★ ★ ★

Landon recovered Golbek's pistol. It was a black, self-loader of German origin, with four rounds left in it. The weather had cleared, and the surface of Delaware Bay was reasonably calm. The main deck of the *Gloria del Mar* was streaked with salt, but the water had all run away. Landon found the pistol wedged under a pipe; he pocketed it quickly, without anyone seeing him, and hunted about for Garcia's weapon. He was unable to find it, however, and came to the conclusion that it must have been washed overboard or retrieved by some one else.

He carried on with his work, and when the crew knocked off for the mid-morning break he took Golbek's pistol to his cabin. He took it to pieces, dried the parts, rubbed them with an oily rag, and put them together again. He reloaded the four cartridges, slipped the safety-catch on, and pushed the pistol into the right-hand pocket of his jacket. After some consideration, however, he decided that it made too much of a bulge; he took it out again, opened the drawer under his bunk, hid the pistol under a layer of clothing, and kicked the drawer shut again.

He supposed it was possible that both Golbek and Garcia were now unarmed; but he could not be sure. They might well have had more than one gun apiece; he did not know how big an armoury they carried about with them, and he could not be certain that Garcia had not recovered his own pistol early in the morning.

Of one thing only did he feel absolutely certain: that the failure of the previous night would not cause the two to give up their attempts to prevent his escaping with the letter for Mr Delgado. With the ship now so close to land they were likely to become all the more desperate. He must still be as vigilant as ever.

There was an American pilot on board now, a stout, cigar-chewing Philadelphian, wearing a sheepskin coat and a fur cap with ear-flaps. Hearing the nasal Yankee voice as he did his trick at the wheel, Landon felt curiously encouraged. It was as though this sturdy, capable individual were a symbol of law and order — of protection from the killer, Golbek. He felt a desire to turn to the man and tell him about Garcia and Golbek, and to ask for his help. The idea was, of course, ridiculous. Even if this man had been an American policeman or a member of the F.B.I., he could have expected no help from that quarter, for he was himself outside the law, a fugitive from a South American gaol, with perhaps the charge of killing a man levelled against him. He felt again a sense of loneliness, the loneliness of Ishmael, the outcast.

The *Gloria del Mar* came to the end of her voyage under the shadow of the great tanks and towers of the refinery, beside a maze of pipes and pumping-machinery, of gantries and steel ladders, of shining metal and bright paint. Here, where the crude petroleum that the earth had yielded would be broken down into its many products, the ship was made fast by steel hawsers and mooring-ropes, and the fat black pipes were rigged for discharge.

The decks were slippery with ice and snow, and a great sheet of hard-packed ice covered the oil-wharf. The sky was lead-coloured, and the temperature was reaching down towards the zero mark.

Landon was already thinking about getting ashore and catching the train for New York. Mr Delgado, five thousand dollars, Gloria Swindon — his thoughts moved along the links of that chain. It was Green who told him that there was no chance of getting ashore before the following day.

"It's the usual formalities with officials. There'll be no shore passes until to-morrow."

"Isn't there any way of speeding things up? I don't want to be here for another night."

"If you're ready to knock down a few policemen you might make it. Can't see how else. These people are hospitable enough when you get to know them, but they don't let just anybody set foot on the sacred soil of freedom."

Landon had been ready to go, waiting for the starter's gun; but it was no good. Even if he managed to leave the ship without a pass, he would never be able to get beyond the limits of the refinery. There was nothing for it but to be patient for a little while longer, patient and watchful.

He had seen nothing of Garcia since the shooting incident, and he had caught only a fleeting glimpse of Golbek. Golbek had a dark bruise on his right cheek and a bandage round his left wrist. He appeared to be walking lame, but it was difficult to tell for certain whether this were so, for he had always had such a dragging, shuffling step that an extra limp made little difference.

He and Landon passed each other so closely that they might have touched hands, but, as usual, there was a complete lack of expression on Golbek's face; Landon might have been a stranger passing him by in the street. He did not avert his gaze; his cold, stony eyes simply stared at Landon, at and through him, as though he did not exist. Landon caught a whiff of scent, and felt, as ever, a creeping of the skin from the very presence of this toad-like creature. There was something strangely unnatural in this passing by without a word, without so much as a flicker of recognition from this man who had tried to kill him, and would undoubtedly try again if given the smallest chance. He wondered whether Golbek had another gun, but it was impossible to tell.

Landon and Green slept with the cabin door locked and the porthole cover screwed down; but the night passed without incident. It was the following mid-day, when the shore passes were being issued, that Landon received a shock: there was to be no pass for him. He approached the mate, but that taciturn man simply raised his shoulders in a gesture of refusal to take any responsibility for the state of affairs.

"It is nothing to do with me. It is the immigration authorities; they refuse to issue a permit. They do not wish you to land. You are what they call undesirable. They have information perhaps. It is nothing to me. But you cannot go ashore."

Landon went back to his own quarters, thinking hard. He supposed some report concerning him must have come through from the Central Republic. Though the United States police might not arrest him, they obviously meant to see that he caused no trouble in their country. He was in a tight corner now. With no pass he could not get ashore, and if he did not get ashore he certainly could not contact Mr Delgado, pick up the five thousand dollars, and find Gloria Swindon. It was the devil.

When he came to the after end of the cat-walk he had another shock. Looking up towards the poop-deck, where the lifeboats were carried, he saw that the boat in which he had hidden Delgado's letter had had its canvas cover stripped off. In a moment he was up the ladder and running towards the boat. Suppose the letter had been discovered? Suppose it had been taken away? Suppose it was even now in the fat hands of Captain Garcia?

He saw that there was a man in the boat — a stranger to him — and that he was pulling out the stores and piling them on the thwarts. Landon rested his hands on the gunwale of the boat and with an effort managed to keep his voice calm.

"What are you doing?"

The man looked up. He pushed his leather cap to the back of his head and squinted at Landon through a pair of rimless glasses.

"Hi there, feller! You speak English?"

"I am English," Landon said.

"That so? A Limey, huh? How's the world treating you?"

"So, so. What's the great idea — pulling the guts out of the boat?

"Just a routine check-up. Changing the

stores. Got to be done some time. You bin on this hooker long?"

"Not long," Landon said. "I was in South America. I signed on in Buenos Aires."

"Fine place, so I've heard tell." The American sat down on one of the thwarts and felt in his pocket for a stick of chewing-gum. He seemed talkative. "I guess you had a swell time down there. Me, I've never been south of Florida. Some day maybe I get myself a ticket for Rio. " He began to chew, thinking perhaps of a Brazilian holiday — some day."

Landon could see the canvas-wrapped package in which he had hidden his letter. He could have touched it by stretching out his hand, but he had to move warily. This man seemed friendly enough, but that was not to say that he would allow Landon to rummage the stores.

He said: "What are you going to do with the old stores?"

"Take 'em away. There's the new lot on the deck there."

Landon pointed to the package in

301

which the letter was concealed. "That too?"

"Sure, sure." The man looked at him, suddenly suspicious. "Look, Mac; what makes you so interested in this junk? You got shares in it or sumpin?"

Landon thought swiftly. If the stores were taken away there would be little hope of recovering the letter. He had been a fool not to have removed it already, but it had appeared to him to be safe enough in the lifeboat. That the lifeboat might be overhauled had simply not occurred to him.

He decided to take the lesser risk, to tell this man the truth — or at least part of the truth. The fellow appeared to be reasonable.

"The fact is," he said, "I've got something in that package. An envelope. I slipped it under the canvas for safekeeping. I'd hate to lose it."

The man grinned, and Landon realized that he need not have worried.

"Photos?"

"Photos? Yes — yes, that's it — photos."

"Hot ones, I bet. Well, well, that was a good place to hide them. Don't suppose the customs guys would look in there. Filthy pictures, huh? Well, you better take 'em — quick."

He pushed the package towards Landon and watched while Landon rapidly untied the cord and slipped the oilcloth-covered envelope out of its hiding-place. His eyes seemed to gleam a little behind the glasses as Landon pushed the thin parcel into his inner pocket.

"How about giving a guy a peek?" he said.

"I'm sorry," Landon said. "They're sealed up."

The American seemed disappointed. "That sure is a pity. You couldn't mebbe break the seal?"

"I'm afraid not," Landon said. "I've got to deliver them as they are. If the seal is broken — no money for me. You see how it is?"

"I see how it is. But it sure seems a pity."

"I'm sorry," Landon said again. "Thanks for the help, though."

"Don't give it a thought," the man said.

Landon buttoned up his coat and

walked to the head of the ladder leading to the deck below. He was about to descend when he looked over his shoulder and saw Golbek standing motionless by the after rails, staring at him.

# 17

## Broken Sleep

"SO they won't give you a pass," Green said. "They got wind of something, maybe."

"Maybe," Landon said. "Anyway, it seems I'm *persona non grata* with the American authorities."

"Is that something bad? It sounds like it."

"Bad enough to make it confoundedly difficult to get ashore. They're pretty watchful in places like this."

Green was dressing in his best shore-going clothes — a blue pin-stripe suit, pointed yellow shoes, a polka-dot shirt, and a tie with the picture of a nude woman painted on it. No difficulties had been raised in the matter of his pass.

"Do you think Garcia queered your pitch with the F.B.I.?" he asked. "He may have told them something just to keep you on board."

Landon shook his head. "If you ask me this has nothing to do with our friend Garcia. I don't think he would be too keen on taking the Yankee police into his confidence; he has other methods of working. No; I fancy this information came through by some other route."

"What are you going to do?"

"I'll have to think of something."

Green looped a silver chain across his tie. He began to comb his hair.

"You wouldn't like me to deliver the letter for you? I could nip up to New York and get back before the ship sails. I could bring the cash back with me."

"No," Landon said. "I've got to see Mr Delgado myself; that was the contract."

"You can trust me. I wouldn't scoot with the dough."

"I know you wouldn't. Don't think I'm afraid of that. But I promised to give the letter personally into the hand of Mr Delgado and not to let anyone else have it, whatever happened. Besides which, I have other business in New York. No offence?"

"Hell, no." Green put the comb away in his pocket and shrugged himself into an overcoat. "Well, I'm off. Philadelphia, here I come. Don't sit up for me."

"I won't. You'll be ashore all night, I expect."

"Maybe. And maybe not. It depends on circumstances. You never know what may turn up."

"Don't get too drunk. You've got plenty of dollars?"

Green showed a wad of notes, grinning. "Made a hole in my wages. Hell, what good is it, 'cept to spend?"

He went out of the cabin, leaving Landon to smoke in solitude and try to work out a plan of action. Somehow Landon had to get ashore and on to New York; but without a pass and without dollars that presented a real problem. He wondered what Garcia's next move would be. Did Garcia realize that the Americans were stopping him from going ashore? Was Garcia still on board? He did not even know the answer to that question. He had not seen the supposed Bolivian businessman go ashore, but that did not mean that he had not done so. Presumably he had simply paid for a passage from Venezuela to Philadelphia and would be expected to leave the ship at the end of the voyage. On the other hand, he could easily have thought up some excuse for prolonging his stay on board for a day or two if it should suit his purpose.

Of one thing Landon was certain: Golbek had seen him take the letter from the lifeboat. The chances were that he would make some attempt to obtain it and eliminate Landon with as little delay as possible — probably this very night.

It was seven o'clock. He crushed out the stub of his cigarette and went out on deck. It had begun to snow again, and the flakes, blowing across the beams of the electric lamps, were silhouetted against the dark background of the night like chalk marks drifting across a blackboard. The frost in the air was like a hand gripping the chest. Shivering, Landon made his way to the crew's mess-room. It was deserted, except for McNulty sitting morosely at one end of the long table, sipping cocoa from a big white mug and playing patience.

Landon was surprised to see him. "No shore for you, Paddy?"

McNulty scowled. "And where would be the sense in going ashore with no dollars?"

"Didn't you draw any?"

"I did that. And didn't I go and lose the lot of it to that cheating swine of a bosun?"

"You mean to say you were damn fool enough to play cards with Schmidt again? I thought you'd had enough of that sort of business."

"Not cards," McNulty said. "Dice."

"And he skinned you out?"

"He did. And now he's gone ashore to spend my money, damn his bloody eyes."

Landon made himself a cup of cocoa. He was not sorry to have McNulty's company. There was something strangely gloomy about the almost deserted ship. Without its crew a ship was a dead thing, echoing hollowly to any sound. Somewhere Golbek was waiting. For what? Landon began to wish that he had finished with Golbek once and for all while the ship had been at sea. It had been possible then. Instead, Golbek was still very much alive, still a killer, still with old scores to settle and his contract to fulfil.

McNulty said: "You staying aboard, too?"

"Yes."

McNulty brightened a little. "Play cards?"

"What for?"

"I got a few pesos left."

Landon played cards with McNulty until almost midnight. Altogether he lost sixty-five centavos. He would have gone on playing, but McNulty had had enough.

"It's me for the bunk now." He stood up, stretched himself, and yawned. He peered at the dark circle of one of the portholes, on the outer rim of which a white arc of snow had collected. They could hear the wind whining. "Sure, it's the wild night and all. Maybe we're better on board, anyway. Ah well, let's be going and losing ourselves in the sweet arms o' Morpheus."

He gave a little jerk of his head, by way of a gesture of good-night, and went out of the mess-room, a man, like Landon, totally alone in the world; a wizened, wrinkled man who had sailed the high seas for perhaps forty years of his life and had no friends anywhere — only the brief comradeships of the seamen's mess, always changing, never constant. What would be the end of it for him when he was no longer able to carry out the tasks of an able-bodied seaman, when he was too old to be of any further use to a ship? What future was there for him? Would he perhaps walk overboard on some dark night and find oblivion in that sea which he had served so long?

Landon wished that McNulty had not gone. The room seemed lonely now, with its long mess-table and the rows of empty chairs, like a house once loud with laughter and voices, now deserted but for one last survivor. He listened to the doleful sound of the wind, and wondered where Golbek was. He shivered. Damn it; he was allowing the fellow to play on his nerves. If he didn't take a grip on himself he would be jumping at every shadow.

He decided to go to his cabin and try to get some sleep. Outside, the snow seemed to be falling faster. Down by the gangway under the white light of the electric lamp he could see a policeman beating his hands, the snow caking on his shoulders. Did those people never sleep? His gaze moved on towards the dark mass of the midships deck-house, scarcely visible through the drifting curtain of snow. Was Garcia there? Was Golbek awake? He could not tell.

He went to his cabin, his feet sinking into the soft snow on the deck. He went inside, switched the light on, and shut and locked the door. He drew the curtain across the porthole, and then kicked off his gumboots and took off his jacket. He switched the light off and lay down on the lower bunk.

He could not bring himself to undress completely, feeling somehow that to do so would be to lower his guard, to leave himself open to attack. For a long time he lay in the darkness, smoking and listening to the moaning of the wind. A dozen times he fancied that he heard other sounds — the scuffle of footsteps in the snow, the scratching of fingers on the door, the low whisper of men's voices. But he was tired, and his eyelids were leaden; he knew that all these sounds were no more than the conjurings of imagination, the products of his own fears.

He did not know how long he slept. When he awoke the cabin was still in darkness, and the wind was still moaning outside. He had no watch to tell him what time it was, but his mouth felt dry and parched, as though he had been on a long journey through a waterless desert. His tongue felt like leather; perhaps it was the result of smoking too many cigarettes. Whatever it was, he needed a drink. He thought of the mess-room where he could make himself a cup of coffee, and he could almost taste the sweetness and the tang of it. But to get to the mess-room he would have to leave the safety of his cabin, this secure little cell inside which he had locked himself. He would have to risk encountering Golbek, and perhaps Garcia as well.

He thought of this and he thought of the coffee. And then he felt angry with himself for allowing the fear of Golbek to keep him skulking in his cabin — the toad-like Golbek, who was probably at this moment asleep in his bunk amidships.

Landon got up, found his jacket and gumboots in the darkness, and pulled them on. He did not switch the light on, but he pulled open the drawer under his bunk, rummaged among the clothes, and felt the cold, hard surface of the self-loading pistol under his fingers. He slipped it into his jacket pocket, unlocked the cabin door, and went out into the night.

The snow had stopped falling, and there was a frosty brilliance in the lamps showing here and there about the ship and the refinery; they glittered, sending out long spears of light, like luminous splinters of ice pricking into the darkness. Landon did not waste time; the cold was vicious. He went through the deck-house doorway, down the short alleyway, and into the mess-room.

As he crossed the threshold he thought he heard a sound as of a man drawing breath sharply, and he reached suddenly for the gun in his pocket. But when he switched the light on he saw that the mess-room was deserted. He shut the door and pushed a chair under the knob, jamming it.

He made coffee with water from the electric boiler over the sink, stirred in sugar and condensed milk, and sat down at the end of the table farthest from the door. The coffee tasted good; it eased the hard, dry feeling of his tongue and unclogged his throat. He took a second cup and lit a cigarette. There was a brass clock screwed to the bulkhead over the door; it showed that the time was a quarter past three.

Landon smoked the cigarette slowly, listening to the wind and the small, furtive sounds that came from inside the ship — unaccountable sounds like those one hears in an empty house. His eyelids felt heavy with sleep. He leaned forward on the table and rested his head on his hands.

He had not meant to sleep, but when he suddenly awoke and raised his head he saw that the cigarette had burnt itself out on the table where he had laid it, leaving a little cylinder of cold ash. He looked up at the clock; it was nearly four.

He knew what it was that had awakened him: there was a grumbling in his belly, a sensation as of long fingers groping softly for a hold. It was the old wound starting to play its tricks again, the iron preparing for a new attack.

He got up heavily from the chair. Soon the pain would really be on him, and he did not want to face it here; he wanted to be on his bunk, where he could thrust his face into the pillow, smothering his agony. He pulled the chair away from the mess-room door and went out into the alley-way. He had almost forgotten Golbek, for when the pain came it swamped all else, and he could think of nothing but the task of fighting the devil inside him.

He went out to the deck, crossed through the soft snow to the starboard side, and went into his own cabin. He shut the door behind him, and as he did so a wave of fear swept over him, stronger even than the pain in his belly. In the darkness was an unmistakable sweet, sickly odour — Golbek's scent.

For a few moments Landon stood with his back pressed against the door, breathing rapidly as though after some fierce physical exertion. He knew that Golbek was in the cabin, waiting silently in the darkness. The thought seemed to paralyse Landon, to deprive his limbs of their power, to freeze his brain, so that he could not think what action to take, could think of nothing but the overpowering, nauseating odour of Golbek's scent.

In the cabin there was absolute silence, but for the sound of Landon's own breathing. Outside the wind howled; inside nothing moved. Landon's brain began to work again. He slipped his hand gently into his jacket pocket and gripped the self-loading pistol. With his thumb he eased back the safety-catch and drew the pistol softly from his pocket.

Holding the pistol ready in his right hand, he groped with his other hand for the switch of the electric light. He found it and flicked the light on. The cabin was empty, but for himself and a man lying face downward on the lower bunk.

The man appeared to be sleeping soundly. He did not move when the light came on. Landon stepped towards the bunk and saw why he did not move, why he would never move again. From between his shoulder-blades the hilt of a knife protruded like a black stake.

# 18

## The Pay-off

IT was Jonas Green, still fully dressed in his shore-going clothes. His overcoat was lying on the floor, and it was obvious to Landon that he had come in fuddled with drink and, after peeling off the coat, had flung himself down on the lower bunk — the one it was easier to climb on to. Into Landon's mind came the words that Green had used when the question of choice of bunks had arisen: 'Call it superstition if you like, but I reckon it's unlucky for me to sleep in a bottom bunk . . . ' Superstition or not, he had been right. And now he would never sleep in a top bunk again, never drive a winch, never splice a rope, never do another trick at the wheel. It was all finished — finished by a thin, sharp knife driven in between the shoulder-blades.

"You poor devil!" Landon muttered. "You poor, damned unlucky devil!" For he knew that the knife thrust so deep into Green's back had been meant for him, Landon — that it had been plunged quickly home before the mistake could be discovered. And the scent told him that it had been Golbek who had done the thrusting.

Green's shoes were still on his feet, and the snow, melting from them, had soaked into the bed-cover, leaving on it a wet, dirty mark. His longish hair had flopped forward over the pillow in an untidy mass, and his hands, one on either side of his head, were grasping the pillow, as if in the sudden convulsion of death.

Yet signs of death and violence were strangely lacking. There was no blood; any haemorrhage there might have been had been internal. The knife had gone cleanly in up to the hilt, so that the handle protruding from Green's back might have been some peculiar attachment to his jacket rather than the visible part of a lethal weapon.

Landon touched the back of Greens, head. The neck was still warm; it seemed hard to believe that the life had fled from it. A wave of pity swept through Landon, then, immediately following it, a wave of anger so fierce that it made him shiver. Golbek had done this — that creeping toad-like creature, that half-man, that swine, that treacherous, murdering bastard. Why should it have been in the power of such a wretch to end the life of a decent fellow like Green?

"Damn him!" Landon muttered. "Damn his filthy, stinking hide!"

He heard the cabin door open, and he swung round, bringing up his right hand with the pistol in it. But the revolver pointing at him from the hands of Captain Garcia did not waver. "Drop your gun," Garcia said.

Landon hesitated, the pistol half up.

"Drop it!"

Landon dropped the pistol, and it fell with a clang on the red-painted iron of the cabin floor. Garcia had the advantage; before Landon could have used his own gun Garcia would have shot him.

"That was wise," Garcia said. He advanced farther into the cabin, and Golbek came in at his heels like a dog behind its master. Golbek shut the door; he appeared to be unarmed.

"Murdering swine!" Landon said.

Garcia's eyes flickered for a moment towards the bunk on which Green's motionless body lay. "That! It was a foolish mistake. Henryk was over-hasty. We had nothing against that man; it was unfortunate for him that he should have been in the wrong place at the wrong time. It was not my intention that he should be killed."

"The knife was meant for me."

"Exactly. For you. Really, Señor Landon, you are a most fortunate man. You have escaped death by so narrow a margin on so many occasions that one might almost fancy you had a charmed life. Has that idea occurred to you?"

"Talk!" Landon said harshly. "More damned talk! Get on with it. What method have you decided on for my execution?"

He could see Golbek, with his bruised face, standing silently behind Garcia; Golbek, with his cold killer's eyes, quite unmoved by the fact that he had so recently murdered a man — that the body

322

was lying there still, accusing him. Golbek knew no such emotion as remorse. And when the time came to do so he would kill Landon with as little compunction, without pity, and with only a strange, unnatural exultation. For Landon knew that there was no intention of letting him escape. The only question was, why had they not killed him at once? Why was Garcia delaying? Was it simply to torture him?

He felt the pain, momentarily forgotten, begin again to grumble in his belly, and he yelled at Garcia: "Why don't you kill me too? What are you waiting for? Do the stars have to be propitious? Do you have to do it at a certain hour?"

"What makes you so certain that we shall kill you?" Garcia asked.

"What should make me think you won't? What else have you come here for?"

Garcia said smoothly: "You misjudge me. I have told you before that I detest killing. It is a necessity at times, but I detest it. Believe me, I do not wish to kill you. Nor need the necessity arise even now if you will only be reasonable, if you will only act with good sense."

"What do you mean by that?"

"If you will give me the letter you have for Señor Delgado, the letter you hid in the lifeboat."

So that was it. Landon now saw clearly why Garcia was parleying. Golbek had obviously told him what he had seen. Garcia knew that Landon had the letter again, but he could not be certain that he had not rehidden it in some other place; he could not be sure that it was in Landon's pocket. Garcia badly wanted that letter; if he killed Landon before finding it he might lose it for ever. Admittedly Green had been killed without hesitation, but that might well have been the result of unchecked impetuosity on the part of Henryk Golbek. Landon had a feeling that Golbek did not really care two pins about the letter, but that he was only interested in killing. Garcia, on the other hand, did care about it; he cared very much. Therefore he was perfectly willing to offer Landon his life in exchange for the letter, knowing that he need not keep his side of such a bargain.

Landon was not fool enough to believe that he could save his life by this method. They would kill him whether he gave up the letter or not; to hand it over would merely be to save Garcia the trouble of hunting for it. It was ridiculous to suppose that Garcia would let him go free to tell all that he knew about the death of Green. Even if there had been any hope of mercy in the first place — which was doubtful — that hope had most certainly withered away now.

"Come," Garcia said in the tone of a reasonable man, willing to make concessions. "I have never borne you any ill will. I am sure we can come to an amiable agreement."

"At the point of a gun?"

Garcia smiled, but he did not lower the revolver. "You are an impetuous man. I fear it might be imprudent of me to take any risk."

Behind him Golbek leaned against the door, apparently taking no interest in what was going on, his pallid face empty as always of any expression, his moist lower lip hanging loosely, a lock of damp, mouse-coloured hair falling over his forehead. Perhaps Garcia was telling the truth when he protested that he disliked killing — that he disliked doing the job himself, at least. But he had his killer with him. Golbek was the one to do the dirty work. Perhaps he had another knife; it would be more silent than a gun.

Garcia began to lose patience. His voice hardened slightly. "I cannot wait for ever. Do not be a fool, Landon. Tell me where the letter is. You do not help yourself by being stubborn. You will die, and then we shall find the letter afterwards; it is all one to me."

"Except that you do not like killing," Landon said sardonically. "You have surely not forgotten your Christian principles so quickly."

Garcia's face darkened; he did not care for being laughed at. "I ask you once more — will you give up the letter? I give you ten seconds to answer yes or no."

"No," Landon shouted. And then the pain wrenched at his belly as he had never felt it before. It was unbearable. He screamed once, and the pain dragged him down, doubling up his body like a jack-knife.

He heard the explosion of Garcia's revolver, so close as to be almost deafening, and he felt the blast of it scorching a furrow through his hair. Then he had his arms round Garcia's legs and with a great heave flung him on to his back. With anger and the pain in his body like twin devils, he seized Garcia's neck and began to beat his head furiously against the iron floor, trying to beat the pain out of his own belly, the pain that was making him mad, hardly caring whether he lived or died, since life could only mean successive bouts of this tearing, raging anguish of the belly.

He saw Golbek lunge at him, and he rolled to one side with a convulsive jerk of the body. Golbek's knife slithered into the flesh under his left armpit, just missing the ribs. With his right hand he found the pistol he had dropped — Golbek's pistol. He swung it up, rammed the barrel into Golbek's mouth, and pressed the trigger.

Golbek's body fell twitching across Garcia's face. Garcia pushed it to one side and sat up, Golbek's blood streaming down his cheeks. He still had the revolver in his hand, but he did not have a chance to use it. Landon shot him between the eyes.

Then the pain tore at Landon, flailed him. He had just killed two men, and he could think of nothing but the iron talons clawing at his belly. He sat on the settee, doubled up with pain, not caring whether anyone had heard the shots, or whether anyone would come running to the cabin to find three dead men and a fourth writhing in agony.

But no one came, and gradually the pain subsided, leaving him weak and gasping, but able to think clearly again and to consider his position. He could feel blood from the knife-wound that Golbek had inflicted soaking into his shirt. He took off his jacket; there was a rent in it where the knife had slit the cloth, but it was nothing. He removed his sweater and found the shirt beneath red with blood. He took off the shirt and wiped the wound. The blood had made it appear worse that it really was — a clean cut about four inches long, not deep. He found some more of the plaster that Green had used on his forearm and covered the cut. He put on a clean shirt and began to pack his suitcase.

The bodies of Golbek and Garcia were in his way; he kept stumbling over them. He removed the watch from Garcia's wrist and strapped it in its rightful place on his own. Then he dragged the bodies to one side of the cabin and covered them with a blanket.

When he had packed his suitcase he put on his sweater and jacket and changed his gumboots for a pair of leather shoes. Then he rolled Green's body over on to one side, so that he could get at the inner pocket of his jacket, and felt inside for his wallet. He was relieved to find it there, and to discover that it still contained a thick wad of dollar bills, together with Green's shore pass. Landon put the wallet and the pass in his own pocket, pulled on his oilskin coat, picked up the suitcase, switched off the cabin light, and went outside. He took the key from the inside of the door, shut and locked the door, and threw the key into the dock.

He felt weak and worn out, as he

always did after a bout with his old wound. It was as if he had just emerged from a twenty-round contest; he felt tired, bruised, beaten.

The wind, which had veered round more to the east, struck him in the face like a spear of ice. It was still dark, but he knew that before very long the grey light of morning would be creeping in from the east, and that the ship would come to life again. Before that time he had to be on his way. He must not wait for the daylight to catch him.

But first he had to wash the blood off his hands. He went through the doorway into the crew's alley-way, put down his suitcase just inside the door, and walked to the wash-place. There was blood all over his hands; he turned on the hot-water tap and rubbed them with soap, letting the water flow over them. The blood came off reluctantly, slimily; but he had not the time to be too particular. He dried his hands on a roller towel and glanced at his face in a mirror. He took no pleasure in what he saw reflected there — a thin, sick-looking face with prominent bones, darkened with beard stubble and hollow-eyed.

He walked out of the wash-place and ran straight into Hermann Schmidt.

Schmidt was drunk; there could be no doubt about that. He was swaying on his feet, as if to counteract a non-existent roll of the ship; his scarred face glowed like a furnace door, and there was a bruise over his right eye that seemed to indicate a recent fight. But he was not too drunk to recognize Landon. He grabbed Landon's arm with one of his massive, steel-claw hands.

"My frien', my dear frien'. How glad I find you! You come to my cabin now. Ve drink."

Landon tried to drag his arms away, but the bosun's grip tightened.

"I have visky — two bottle. Rye visky. Goot." He tapped one of the pockets of his coat, and a bottle clinked. "Come now. Ve let bygones be bygones an' drink together."

In liquor Schmidt had become over-poweringly friendly. He swayed in front of Landon, breathing out alcohol like a distillery. There was water in his piggy eyes — perhaps tears. Landon cursed the ill chance that had brought this encounter upon him at such a moment. Two minutes later and Schmidt would have been gone to his cabin; the way would have been clear.

He said: "I'm sorry, bosun. Not just now. I'm in a hurry."

"Vot hurry! No gottam hurry. I say you drink vith me. No man refuse a drink with Hermann Schmidt. Blutty hell! Vot is wrong with you? Are you sick? Can't you drink a glass of goot liquor, hey?"

His mood was changing to one of aggression, and he had raised his voice. Landon was afraid the noise might awaken others of the crew and attract even more undesirable attention. There was no getting away; Schmidt stood squarely across the line of escape, and for all his drunkenness his grip on Landon's arm was powerful. And Landon felt weak. Perhaps, after all, a shot of whisky might do him good.

"All right," he said. "I'll have a drink with you."

"Course you vill. No nonsense, eh? A blutty goot drink of visky never done nobody no damn harm."

Schmidt's cabin was small and hot. Landon sat on the bunk while Schmidt dragged two bottles of rye whisky out of his pockets, found one glass tumbler and one cracked teacup without a handle, and poured whisky into each of these receptacles. Magnanimously he allowed Landon to have the glass and took the cup for himself.

"Drink it down."

Landon drank. The whisky was fiery, but not so bad as the so-called Scotch he had drunk in Buenos Aires. He could feel the trail of warmth reaching down towards his stomach. Schmidt drained the cup and poured two more tots. Landon noticed that for a man so obviously drunk his hand was remarkably steady when pouring drinks; perhaps he had some special control that made sure he did not waste valuable liquor by spilling it.

"You an' me," Schmidt said, gazing at Landon over the chipped rim of his cup; "you an' me blutty goot frien's now. No more fights, hey? Vot you say?"

"It suits me," Landon said. He was wondering how soon he could get away. Schmidt was in a brotherly mood, but the balance between friendliness and anger was delicate. To walk out on him now might be to throw him into uncontrollable rage; he might become violent and abusive, noisy enough to rouse others in the ship.

Yet time was passing, valuable minutes of darkness were slipping away, and in a cabin only a few yards from the bosun's three dead men were lying, waiting to be discovered. Landon was threatened by two dangers — the danger of angering Schmidt and the danger of losing time. He glanced at the watch on his wrist, the watch he had at last regained from Garcia. Already the hands were drawing towards five o'clock. Soon the cook would be getting busy in the galley; men would be stirring; the ship would be waking up to a new day.

Schmidt began to talk. "You English and us Germans, ve ought never to fight each others. Ve are brother nations. Together, vot ve not able to do? Ve could conquer the whole vorld. Frenchmen, Russians, Italians, Jews, Greeks — all scum." He leaned towards Landon, his pale, watery eyes trying to focus, a film

334

of sweat on his upper lip. "There is only two nations is vorth anything — mine an' yours. Vy then must ve fight each other? Together ve could have the vip hand — the vip. Is not so?" He gripped the cup in his right hand, as though it were indeed the butt of a whip, and so tightly that at any moment Landon expected to see it break into pieces.

Schmidt took a sip of whisky. "To vip the scum is goot. I have vipped much in the goot old days. Other things I do, too. It is goot then, blooty goot."

"When the Nazis were in power," Landon said. There must have been more than a hint of disgust in his voice, for Schmidt's head jerked a little, and he stared at Landon suspiciously. Perhaps he was not so drunk that he could not detect antagonism.

"Yes, that is so. Perhaps you do not like — Nazis. Perhaps you think you high and blutty mighty." His voice was rising again. "Perhaps you think you too blutty superior to be frien's with a German — a Nazi. Is not so?"

Landon spoke soothingly. "Not at all. I am very pleased to be your friend. I

335

am honoured." The irony with which the last words were uttered did not register on Schmidt. He took them at their face value.

"Goot. That is goot. Now ve drink some more."

"No," Landon said. "No more for me. I've got to go."

"That all blutty nonsense. Vy you have to go?" For the first time Schmidt appeared to notice Landon's oilskin coat. He became suspicious. "Vere you have to go? Is not time to go ashore. Vere you go, hey?"

"Nowhere," Landon said. "Let's have that other drink."

He held out his glass and waited as Schmidt poured whisky into it. He had no wish to drink any more. Above all things he needed to keep a clear head. But Schmidt in his present mood was a difficult man to deal with, ready to take offence in a moment and fly into a rage.

Meanwhile the minutes were ticking remorselessly away, and soon the light would be coming up from the sea, creeping greyly across the land. He had to be away from the ship before then.

Schmidt's eyes blinked. His head dropped forward, the chin resting on his barrel of a chest. For a moment he seemed to doze. But then his head came up again, his eyes opened, and he took a long swig of whisky.

"I tell you a story," he said. "Funny story — 'bout some Jews in Hamburg — in 1933. Gott's blutt! You laugh ven I tell you vot those Jews are made to do . . ."

Landon listened, but he did not laugh. The minutes were slipping away.

"Ve use wire for that job," Schmidt said. "Piano vire, you know. Ve are musical nation, eh? Twist it, an' it cut. Twist it more, an' it cut more . . ."

Schmidt laughed, his eyes closed, dreamy, enjoying the memory of torture inflicted on others — on an inferior race.

I could kill him now, Landon thought. A knife in his throat. He would bleed to death.

But there had been too much killing already. He listened to Schmidt's thick voice — talking, talking, talking. He waited for the opportunity to make a move.

# 19

## End of the Trail

IT was nearly six o'clock when Schmidt at last fell asleep. Landon went out of the cabin quickly, shutting the door behind him. His suitcase was still where he had left it. He picked it up and went out into the cold, clear air of the early morning.

The electric lamp over the gangway was swinging in the wind, its metal hood clanging against the stanchion from which it was hung. Shadows flickered on the snow.

There were no policemen at the gangway. Landon walked down it, his feet slipping in the snow, one hand on the rail to steady himself. Lamps here and there spilled light on to the tall towers of the refinery. Two men came towards Landon, hunched in fleece-lined leather jackets.

"Which way do I get out of this place?" Landon asked.

One of the men jerked a thumb over his shoulder. "Straight down there, Mac. You can't miss."

A bored, sleepy-eyed policeman opened the dock gate to let him through, scarcely troubling to look at the photograph of Jonas Green attached to the pass that Landon showed him. Landon put it away in Green's wallet and stuffed the wallet in his pocket.

"You're away early," the policeman said. He looked at the suitcase. "Any contraband in there?"

Landon grinned. He was feeling better. The whisky had given him confidence. He felt on top of the world. It was almost as if he were already counting the five thousand dollars that Mr Delgado would soon be giving him.

"Take a look if you think so," he said.

"Maybe I will."

Landon opened the case, and the policeman made a rapid search through the clothing inside.

"Okay. On your way, pal."

Landon was lucky with the trains; at ten o'clock he was sitting in an eating-house in New York, filling himself with a big plate of ham and eggs and beans, washed down with hot coffee. With the meal inside him, he went to a barber's shop and had himself shaved. A Negro shoe-shine boy polished his shoes. Landon tossed the boy a coin and saw the brilliant flash of white teeth. "Thank you, suh."

It was now past eleven — time to contact Mr Delgado. He found a subway station and took a down-town train, coming up amid the great concrete cliffs at the southern end of Manhattan Island. He walked down two blocks, counting the numbers, found the building he wanted, and pushed his way in through a revolving door.

He found himself in the super-heated air of a palatial hall, with marble pillars reaching up to the high ceiling. He saw a row of lift doors on the opposite side of the hall, walked across, got into a lift, and asked for the tenth floor.

The lift-boy, staring at the oilskin coat, said: "You expectin' rain?"

Landon said: "I'm expecting a fortune."

"Rich uncle died, huh?"

340

"That's about it."

He came out of the lift into a long, wide corridor, with doors opening off on either side and bearing such legends as 'A.B.C. Finance, Inc.,' 'Western Crushing Mills,' and 'The David Blackhouse Trust.' He saw a man carrying a bundle of papers under his arm and asked him whether he could tell him where Mr Delgado's office was. The man gave Landon a hard look that he failed to understand. Then he said: "Delgado's office? Oh, yeah, yeah. Just along there."

Landon went in the direction indicated and came to a door bearing the lettering, 'A. H. Delgado. South American Exchange.' Glancing over his shoulder, he saw that the man who had directed him had not moved; he was standing in the corridor, watching. When he saw that Landon had noticed him he gave a little wave of the hand, turned, and walked away.

Landon pressed the bell on the office door and waited. After a few moments a middle-aged woman opened the door. She was wearing glasses and had a worried expression, as though much

341

responsibility rested on her unwilling shoulders.

"I wish to see Mr Delgado," Landon said. "I'm afraid I haven't an appointment, but it's very important. I wonder whether I could see him at once."

"No, you can't."

"Isn't he in? When can I see him? I've told you the matter is important."

The woman stared at him, her lips tightening, as if she were having difficultly in keeping herself under control. Landon could see the wrinkles that had begun to age her face like some dried-up system of irrigation channels. There were traces of powder in these depressions that seemed to have drifted there like dust carried by the wind. When she answered her voice sounded resentful, as though she were holding Landon to blame for all her troubles.

"You won't be able to see him — ever. Mr Delgado was shot dead in a barber's chair yesterday afternoon."

She shut the door, and Landon found himself staring stupidly at the polished wood, reading over and over again the meaningless words: 'A. H. Delgado.

South American Exchange.'

Going down in the lift, he did not hear the boy speaking to him. He went out through the revolving door and began to walk without any sense of direction. He was washed up, done for, finished. Now there could no longer be any question of finding Gloria Swindon. What sort of a figure would he cut in his rough seaman's clothes and his oilskin coat, without money and without prospects, a man no doubt already being hunted by the police?

He came to a news-stand, groped in his pocket for coins, and bought a paper. The news-vendor looked at him curiously, but said nothing. The wind was flapping Landon's oilskin coat, slapping it against his legs. It was a cold wind, penetrating icily to the skin. A few flakes of snow had begun to fall.

He went into a drug-store and bought himself a cup of hot coffee. Then he began to read the paper.

Two items of news interested him. One was headed: 'Three men murdered. Gruesome find in cabin of oil-tanker in Philadelphia.' The second seemed to be considered of less importance, for the heading was in smaller type. It read: 'Abortive rising in the Central Republic of South America. Don Diego Vargas executed.'

Landon folded the paper and counted his money. He had exactly six dollars and forty-five cents.

He took the letter that Mr Delgado would never read out of his pocket, struck a match, and lit one corner of it. He held the other end in his hand until the flames reached his fingers; then he dropped the charred envelope to the floor and ground it under his foot.

After awhile he began to laugh quietly, but when he saw that people were staring at him he went out of the drug-store and stood watching the traffic swirling past — the buses, the taxi-cabs, the big, opulent cars.

He had come to the end of the trail. The vein of luck had petered out at last.

## Other titles in the Ulverscroft Large Print Series:

## TO FIGHT THE WILD
### Rod Ansell and Rachel Percy

Lost in uncharted Australian bush, Rod Ansell survived by hunting and trapping wild animals, improvising shelter and using all the bushman's skills he knew.

## COROMANDEL
### Pat Barr

India in the 1830s is a hot, uncomfortable place, where the East India Company still rules. Amelia and her new husband find themselves caught up in the animosities which seethe between the old order and the new.

## THE SMALL PARTY
### Lillian Beckwith

A frightening journey to safety begins for Ruth and her small party as their island is caught up in the dangers of armed insurrection.

## THE WILDERNESS WALK
### Sheila Bishop

Stifling unpleasant memories of a misbegotten romance in Cleave with Lord Francis Aubrey, Lavinia goes on holiday there with her sister. The two women are thrust into a romantic intrigue involving none other than Lord Francis.

## THE RELUCTANT GUEST
### Rosalind Brett

Ann Calvert went to spend a month on a South African farm with Theo Borland and his sister. They both proved to be different from her first idea of them, and there was Storr Peterson — the most disturbing man she had ever met.

## ONE ENCHANTED SUMMER
### Anne Tedlock Brooks

A tale of mystery and romance and a girl who found both during one enchanted summer.